For the luxurious and legendary S.S. *Atlanta* the crossing to Canada in mid-November 1906 is a momentous voyage—a chance to prove she is the fastest liner on the Atlantic Ocean.

For Miss Faye Wainwright, granddaughter of the owner, this is the first time she has travelled alone, and the handsome but enigmatic Captain of the *Atlanta* is the first man she has ever met with such a disturbing power to puzzle and annoy her.

But for Captain Gavin MacManus, whose future career depends on the outcome of the voyage, the responsibility of caring for the spoilt and beautiful Miss Wainwright is just one complication he could well do without!

By the same author in Masquerade:

THE QUEEN'S CAPTAIN
HOSTAGE MOST ROYAL
THE SHADOW QUEEN

Perilous
Voyage

Margaret Hope

MILLS & BOON LIMITED
London · Sydney · Toronto

First published in Great Britain 1983 by
Mills & Boon Limited, 15–16 Brook's Mews,
London W1A 1DR

ISBN 0 263 74382 9

Set in 10/10 pt Linotron Times
04/0983

Photoset by Rowland Phototypesetting Ltd
Bury St Edmunds, Suffolk
Made and printed in Great Britain by
Cox & Wyman Ltd, Reading, Berks.

For Peggy and Roy Cramb

CHAPTER
ONE

TRANSFORMED by the pearly dusk of a November afternoon, the *SS Atlanta*, a sea monster of steel and iron, held the centre of the quayside. Although past her first flush of youth, the legendary 'palace of the Atlantic' still attracted large crowds at sailing time, and passengers deemed it an honour to voyage upon her, a proud boast which also cost a great deal of money.

The rich and famous had been arriving in a steady stream, a constant entertainment for the curious. Now two white Mercedes honked their way slowly along the crowded embarkation quay. Hoping for a glimpse of Royalty, at least, children were held aloft, for in 1906 the horseless carriage was still one of the wonders of the modern world.

A girl, swathed in furs, descended from the first automobile, followed by her maid.

'Who is *she*?'

''Spect she's Royalty—cor', look at all that baggage—'

'A Princess, did you say?'

'Like as not.'

The object of their comments beheld their faces as a distant blur. Born and bred to put a brave face upon all occasions, today she was afraid. Her hand trembled on the rail so that she misjudged the gangway step and she was gratefully aware of her maid's steadying hand.

''Pon my soul,' said a voice, better-informed. 'I do believe it's the Wainwright gel.'

Faye Wainwright, it was indeed. And having survived the first hazards of the gangway, she became aware of a shadowy figure in uniform, framed in the archway above. She blinked, trying to get him into focus, instinct alone telling her that his face was stern and unyielding.

Captain Gavin MacManus, commander of the *Atlanta*, was very angry. Fortunately, Faye was totally unaware of the frown of disapproval with which he regarded her apparently endless tide of luggage presently being unloaded from the second Mercedes. Eighteen —nineteen—twenty, he counted. Where was all *that* to be stowed? Surely she—or her grandfather, Sir Joshua—could have advised her that even in staterooms, closet space was not unlimited.

For Captain MacManus, this was the final irritation of a nerve-racking day. At the best of times, he was not a patient man and here he was holding back his ship for this slip of a girl. He was unimpressed by the expensive vision of Arctic fox furs and veils, smiling a shy greeting, or that the face beneath the fur hat was bewitchingly pretty. The gift of poetry bestowed by his Hebridean ancestry was sadly absent or he would have waxed lyrical over the flower-like face of a Dresden china beauty before him. Porcelain skin, shining eyes and rosy lips. Only the Wainwright jawline resembled Sir Joshua, the *Atlanta*'s owner, and suggested that Faye too was descended from generations who had made reputations as fighters, from the Spanish Armada to Trafalgar.

He sighed deeply. The *Atlanta* was his first command. He could well do without the complication of carrying the owner's granddaughter safely across the Atlantic Ocean in weather that promised to be memorable for its severity.

'Welcome aboard, Miss Wainwright. If you will please follow me—'

The Captain was in better focus now and Faye detected a withering glance from piercing eyes that might have splendidly graced a falcon. Indeed, the face before her was that of a hunter: high cheekbones, straight nose slightly curved, generous well-shaped mouth. And unlike the fashion set by King Edward and slavishly followed by men of fashion, the Captain of the *Atlanta* was clean-shaven.

Faye began a conversation about the weather which was brusquely dismissed. How ungracious he was, this tall lean man—and considerably younger than she had been led to expect from her grandfather's description. MacManus had been, for some time, Sir Joshua's first officer and she had imagined a man in the same mould as himself, large and commanding, with a powerful voice and an air of unmistakable authority. Not quite elderly, but distinctly middle-aged—and quite unattractive. But the Captain, she decided, could not be much past thirty and if he were unmarried, which she doubted, his presence must add a considerable flutter in the daydreams of those single or widowed ladies wealthy enough to travel the world, forever casting about with their well-baited matrimonial nets.

'You *are* the Captain?' Even to her own ears, her voice sounded disgracefully accusing, and his contemptuous look turned her face a rosy pink.

'Captain Gavin MacManus, at your service, ma'am.' But there was nothing in the least humble about the bow which accompanied this assurance.

'Am I the last to arrive?' Faye asked, with a breathless shrug, making it sound as if she had run all the way to Southampton and encountered a good many hazards en route.

The Captain tried to keep his temper under control. There were missing supplies to be traced, and some very nervous, irritable and important passengers to be soothed and reassured. As for those poor devils in steerage, the improvements he had recommended to make their quarters a little more bearable had not been carried out.

He looked at the girl before him. Miss Faye Wainwright, a rich spoilt female who did not care a fig for anyone's troubles as long as she was cosseted and comfortable.

'You are the very last, I believe.'

Ignoring obvious disapproval, she smiled up at him, tilting her head on one side in a manner that most men found irresistible. The face of a mischievous angel. 'That is quite all right, Captain. This is *my* ship, you know.' And with this outrageous reminder that he should know *his* place, her imperious gesture indicated that they proceed.

The Captain had very long legs and he now walked fast. Grateful for her maid Simson's arm at her elbow, and terrified that she might stumble or lose sight of the Captain, Faye was more concerned about the direction of her faltering steps than the splendours which surrounded them. Richly-panelled and softly-lit corridors, a monumental staircase where two fluted wings swept down into a grand salon. The sea was totally obliterated from view. The *Atlanta* had ceased to be a luxury liner impatient to set forth across a great ocean. Its opulent interior suggested an English country mansion.

She had not sailed with the *Atlanta* since she was eight, some twelve years since. The decor was new, more luxurious than she remembered. Sumptuous Persian and Indian carpets, handsome tapestries, jostled with mahogany and rosewood furniture; brass and crystal gleamed everywhere.

'And what is that, Captain?' A huge cage with opaque glass walls and gold filigree doors hung suspended between floor and ceiling.

'It is an elevator, ma'am, installed by Sir Joshua to his exact specifications, and designed to assist elderly and infirm passengers who find staircases a trial.'

'It is very small.'

'It is capable of carrying two persons, and is self-operated.'

Faye approved, since it would also be of considerable assistance to short-sighted persons who found stairs a hazard. She made a mental note to have Simmy explain how it worked, since the formidable Captain was already hurrying her towards the owner's stateroom.

Captain MacManus, it so happened, had his own reasons for cordially disliking the elevator. There had been a particularly unpleasant occasion on the last voyage when a Royal Duchess had been trapped, suspended in mid-air. She had screamed—and screamed—for half an hour before she could be released. The memory of it still made the Captain shudder.

At his side, Faye exclaimed pleasantly over the new decor. He tried not to growl answers, to be patient and pleasant as if this were a social occasion and he had all the time in the world. He had his own personal reasons for disliking heiresses, and in particular, spoilt beautiful ones who abandoned love and duty and pined for their earlier cushioned existences.

His silences were not lost upon Faye. She knew too that this was his first command and that he was young indeed to be following the daunting example set by her grandfather. Remembering that Sir Joshua had praised him to her and thought very highly of his capabilities, she wanted suddenly to reassure him—above all, she longed to bring a smile to that stern countenance. A forlorn hope, she decided, for there was little inclination to frivolity in that face which appeared to be composed entirely of angles. Naturally, Grandfather would never have chosen a frivolous man to command his precious *Atlanta*, but did he never laugh? All around them merriment erupted, the joyful sounds of champagne corks and jolly conversations. From half-open cabin doors, rich perfumes mingled with the aromatic fragrance of expensive cigars.

Suddenly Faye was conscious of the blight of bitter loneliness that corrodes the soul itself. She longed to escape, to be part of this anonymous careless jollity.

A door alongside shot open and a man backed into the corridor, laughing loudly. He cannoned into Faye who was precipitated back into the Captain's arms and firmly clasped to his chest, while he endeavoured to protect her from the man's burden of flowers, bottles, plus a small and intensely irritated Pomeranian dog who snapped furiously in everyone's direction.

'Whoops-a-daisy!' Grinning, the intoxicated man steadied himself and apologised.

The Captain tried to be polite, and did not quite succeed. 'Look where you're going, sir', and control that damned dog.'

The maid Simson had rushed forward, tut-tutting and murmuring 'Shouldna' be allowed, dogs on ships,' and anxiously patting Faye's arm: 'Are you all right, Miss Faye—sure?' She treated the encounter with the drunken man like a major disaster.

As they disentangled themselves and proceeded, Faye

discovered that her heart was beating fast. Not because she was disconcerted or upset by the incident, but from quite another cause.

The Captain's close physical presence. Encircled by his arm, his downbent head had touched her brow and she felt as if she had received a sudden shock of electricity. His hand grasped her wrist and it was as if his flesh melted and merged with her own.

Long after they separated and the incident was over, Faye felt confused and embarrassed, as if she bore marks upon her from his unexpected nearness.

She looked at him. Dark, impassive . . . She regarded her own blurred reflection, almost expecting to see evidence of his touch upon her countenance. She need not have feared, for the smooth complexion was unmarked, the soft white skin flawless. Her hands were the same hands, but she shivered in spite of such reassurance. Strange indeed, to feel so indelibly marked by this enigmatic Captain, whose flesh had grazed her own.

He was holding open a door for her. Faye entered and discovered before her a replica of the guest suite at Wainwrights complete to the last detail of Louis Quinze furniture. Through another door, she glimpsed a tall curtained bed.

The Captain mistook her threshold hesitation. 'I trust all is to your satisfaction, ma'am. It is in accordance with Sir Joshua's direct instructions.'

'It is splendid Captain—thank you,' Faye replied, thinking how extraordinarily large and empty the suite seemed for one girl and her maid, even with the huge baskets of flowers and fruit sent to wish her *bon voyage*.

Impatiently, the Captain awaited his dismissal, trying not to indulge his curiosity. The card on the nearest bouquet bore a Royal crest and an indecipherable signature.

'Are you expecting visitors, ma'am?'

Faye shook her head. 'Isn't it rather too late for that? However—'

The Captain was no longer listening to her pleasantries. She had removed her hat as she spoke and he gave an involuntary intake of breath as her hair cascaded

down from its prison. A nimbus of gold, he beheld, the
heavy gold of ripened corn sheaves straight from a
Hebridean harvest. It touched an obscure chord of
memory and the Captain was momentarily nostalgic for
the hearth-fires of his homeland, which he had forsaken
in boyhood to follow a career on the high seas instead of
the poor fishing and crofting his island provided.

Harvest home. Strange that Faye Wainwright should
remind him of that other beloved woman, so different in
every way. Through narrowed eyes, he watched as her
maid rushed forward to take the fur coat she slid from
slim shoulders. A deep blue velvet travelling costume
revealed an exquisitely dainty shape, a full rounded
bosom and a waist he could have spanned with the
fingers of his own strong hands. Fascinated, his eyes
travelled from ruffles of delicate lace caressing a long
slender neck, to the tiny pointed toes of her shoes. He
felt as if she touched his face through the mirror.

Harvest home. What a harvest she would make for
any man to gather into eager arms, for the womanly
smell of a musky exotic perfume followed the movement
of her arms stretched upwards to her hair. An intoxicating fragrance, which threatened to engulf him—

'All visitors ashore, please. All visitors ashore—'

The spell was broken.

'Thank you, Captain Mac—' She realised with horror
that her mind had gone blank.

'MacManus, ma'am.'

'Captain MacMan—us,' she repeated slowly, smiling,
making it sound like a careful experiment in a foreign
language.

The Captain bowed once more and, considering himself dismissed, walked rapidly to the door.

'One moment, if you please, Captain.' Smiling, she
asked: 'You are Scotch?'

He sighed. 'Our whisky is Scotch, Miss Wainwright.
The people who inhabit Scotland are Scottish.' The
addition became a reproof.

Faye ignored a frosty smile. He did not sound in the
least like the Scotsmen she knew and that was why she
had asked the question.

'My maid, Simson, is from Glasgow. Aren't you, Simmy?' Her attempt at informality produced a dour non-committal nod from Simmy, who eyed the Captain with faint hostility as they exchanged a bleak greeting.

Faye bit her lip angrily. She was only trying to be friendly, to break the ice, but this wretched man reduced her to a gauche and awkward schoolgirl, blushing and stammering her responses under his steady unnerving gaze.

She heard herself blundering on, making matters worse. 'You don't sound Scottish at all, you know. Are you really a native of Scotland?' The nervous giggle which accompanied her remark did not amuse Captain MacManus in the least.

'My native tongue, ma'am, is neither Scots nor English. It is the Gaelic. I am Hebridean—from the Western Isles.' Modesty forbore that he should add that the language spoken there was regarded as the purest and most beautiful in the entire world.

'How very interesting.' Faye looked at him, trying desperately to get his face into sharper focus, which left the Captain with an uncomfortable feeling of being reduced to a specimen under a magnifying glass.

It did not improve his temper. Native Scot indeed! Who did she think she was, making him sound as if he should be attired in feathers and warpaint with a bone through his nose? And his blood the purest in the Isles. His forbears had been the High Kings of Ireland who had sailed across to Scotland to Christianise the heathen Picts. His ancestors were already noble chieftains of clans while hers were privateers, scum of the high seas, gaining their favours by toadying to the sly and avaricious Queen Elizabeth of England.

'We're in for rough weather, I gather,' said Faye and the Captain regarded her in surprise. Beyond the port-holes the afternoon sky darkened in a threatening manner while the seabirds screamed and darted in great flurries of white wings. In the Channel this wind would soon reach gale force. A fine beginning to the voyage which in winter was not readily undertaken except by the boldest of travellers, or those whose business interests across the Atlantic left no alternative. He decided the occasion must be very special indeed for Sir Joshua's granddaughter to be permitted to face the ferocity of the Atlantic Ocean in mid-November. Even in summer the crossing could be treacherous for those whose nerves or stomachs were less than robust.

'I suppose we're safe enough aboard the *Atlanta*.' Faye's gesture included the luxurious surroundings of the stateroom. 'However, it isn't all that long ago—is it?—where one out of six ships setting out never reached New York. The graveyard of ships—that's what the sailors used to call it—or so my grandfather tells me.'

Captain MacManus felt that Sir Joshua might have imparted more tactful and soothing information to prepare his granddaughter for the voyage. 'Come now, Miss Wainwright. That was long before our great liners came into being. I assure you they are indestructible—quite impervious to weather and normal hazards. You will be quite safe with us. There is absolutely nothing to fear—just enjoy your voyage and leave us to deal with the weather outside.'

This rather pat speech sounded suspiciously well-rehearsed to Faye's ears. His voice and manner had suddenly acquired reassuring qualities normally reserved for nervous lady passengers.

'I am not in the least afraid, Captain,' she said stiffly, 'there is nothing I enjoy more than a good storm at sea.'

Her irresponsible attitude angered him more than ever and giving a non-committal nod, he prepared once again to leave. Conscious that she had failed again, Faye said to his retreating figure:

'I have never sailed without my grandfather before, Captain MacManus.'

At the door he turned. She suspected a mocking smile twisting his mouth, the only part of that cold face which might decently be described as curved.

'Nor have I, Miss Wainwright. Nor have I!'

The cabin seemed even larger and emptier without him. Only the banks of flowers were left. Faye sighed. The odour of chrysanthemums overwhelmed her with a sense of melancholy, a reminder of the dying of another year. In the silence, she heard sounds of the bustle and call of farewells in the corridor.

Simson had set her silver-topped bottles and hair brushes on the dressing-table in the bedroom, along with a framed photograph of Sir Joshua. Faye regarded it tenderly and whispered:

'I wish—oh I do so wish you were here, dearest Gaffer.'

Sir Joshua had returned from his last voyage on the *Atlanta* a very sick man. Even he had admitted to being really quite ill. Ill enough to turn over command of his beloved ship to the man who had just left Faye's cabin. Faye could scarcely believe that her grandfather was not like other mortals and that he was growing old. He had not missed a single voyage of the *Atlanta* since her first Transatlantic crossing twenty years ago—on a maiden voyage that had brought prestige and fortune to the Wainwright line.

And now he would obey—reluctantly—doctor's orders. Stay ashore, get his land legs again. He would have to rely on young Captain MacManus to test the *Atlanta's* new engines which had just been installed.

Sir Joshua had assured Faye of his restored health although he looked far from fit. She was to visit his old friend Warren Schroeder in Virginia because her grandfather had promised that they would spend Thanksgiving on the tobacco plantation. He refused to listen to Faye's protests. She must go, he had given his word.

'I am to go alone?'

Faye's stricken voice had evoked a brusque but cheery response. She would not be quite alone since Warren Schroeder's sister Dulcie would be joining the *Atlanta* at Halifax and together they would continue to New York where Schroeder waited to escort them to Virginia. There would be racehorses there, the famed Schroeder strain. Horses had been Faye's consolation for the solitary life of one small girl in the empty halls of Wainwrights while her grandfather was at sea.

Horses! She shook her head in bewilderment. Did he not understand that she had long since outgrown a childish passion for horses and ponies and that, of late, her mind had turned to a more enduring kind of human love. `

'Is there something I can get you, Miss Faye?' Aware of distress in her young mistress, Simson hovered, her face anxious.

Faye shook her head and for a moment rested her cheek against Simmy's worn hand. The gesture was one of trust and a deep affection between the two that stemmed from a lifetime's association.

'Everything will be all right, Miss Faye. Just you wait and see. It *will* be.'

'Yes, of course it will.' She mustn't start being sorry for herself. She must look on the bright side, obey Sir Joshua as always. Think of the marvellous holiday awaiting her in Virginia. Think of this voyage, not as a terrifying experience, but as the prelude to another greater adventure.

But the voyage refused to take on reality and her feeling was not enthusiasm, but the ominous dread of trouble ahead. This, she realised, had less to do with bad weather expected than the arrogant Captain Mac-Manus. She had got off to a false start, made a bad impression. With a feeling that he disliked her, disapproved of her, the relationship between them threatened to become increasingly difficult.

It was odd, she thought, regarding her reflection in the mirror. Men normally liked her without the slightest effort on her behalf. Some—a great many—even swore that they loved her.

CHAPTER
TWO

THE *SS Atlanta*'s likeness to Wainwrights did not end with the exterior apartments. The marble bathroom had a sunken bath and gold taps in the shape of fishes. The maid's room was extra spacious for the times and Simson feared she might be called upon to spend a considerable amount of the voyage prostrate upon the comfortable bed provided. Inevitably she would be seasick. She could hardly gaze upon moving water without coming over queasy. Once long ago she had had a sweetheart, a sailor, who had found her disability trying. They had quarrelled and he had disappeared from her life. Sir Joshua assured her that seasickness was nonsense, merely a question of asserting mind over matter. But nothing would—or could—convince Simson.

She stood in the bedroom, her arms full of garments. 'We havena' near enough room for everything, Miss Faye.'

'Just keep the Virginia wardrobe packed meantime.'

'Even so, miss,' Simson eyed the three trunks despairingly. 'Perhaps we could ask the Captain for extra closet space.'

'I think not,' said Faye, mentally conjuring up the Captain's relentless gaze.

'He's just a servant of Sir Joshua's, after all,' Simson reminded her with a contemptuous snort. 'I'm no' afraid of *him*.'

'Nor am I. I'll talk to him at the first opportunity.' But Faye lacked the boldness of her words. Without her grandfather she felt small and vulnerable, lost without his large and reassuring presence, his decisions to lean on.

Guessing the nature of her young mistress's thoughts, Simson thought privately that her employer had shown

less than his usual thoughtfulness in forcing—aye, forcing that was the only word—her beloved wee lass to
undertake such a journey halfway across the world—and
in winter too. A lioness with cubs could not have de-
fended her young more passionately than Simmy. She
had first come to Wainwrights as a nurse with impecc-
able qualifications. Faye was a frail child and needed
constant care, especially as Sir Joshua was away at sea
for a considerable part of each year. The salary he
offered was many times greater than the hospital she
left, where nursing was regarded not as a dedicated
profession, but as little more worthy than domestic
service.

Simson remained at Wainwrights, becoming in due
course lady's maid, companion and home physician. A
useful compendium of roles which Sir Joshua regarded
as infallible qualifications for escorting his dear child
abroad.

Simson never talked about her background, which she
seemed anxious to forget. Faye had learned that she was
one of many children reared in a Glasgow slum. In a
moment of confidence she had hinted that she had been
betrothed briefly to a seafaring man. Her early life did
not concern Sir Joshua. She was reliable, devoted and
completely loyal to the family. She would cheerfully
have laid down her life for Miss Faye and Wainwrights—
in that order.

Now, trying to forget that by tomorrow she would be
facing her enemy, the sea, Simson laid out her mistress's
costumes for approval. At home, the pattern of Faye's
pursuits included tweed jacket and skirt for outdoor
activities, such as riding, which she did most weathers.
Returning to the house, this was exchanged for a loose
morning gown until the luncheon hour where the
fashionable shape demanded rigid corseting. At home,
she would wear a gown of holland or fine wool, while a
luncheon party produced more elaborate concoctions of
velvet, satin or cambric, according to the season and the
occasion. Formal visits brought forth discreet additions
of flowers and feathers.

Faye decided that tweeds would do excellently for

deck activities. Morning gowns were practical, afternoon gowns burst into frills, while full evening dress was Chantilly lace with the inevitable 'dog-collar' made fashionable by Queen Alexandra—a necessity to hide Her Majesty's distressingly scarred neck. Lace was 'the thing'. The King loved to behold ladies in a froth of frills and his wishes were obeyed to the letter and height of extravagant attire.

Simson held out a beribboned afternoon gown in almond satin and lace with matching parasol. 'What about this one, miss?'

'Definitely Virginia,' said Faye. 'I don't see myself promenading in that creation. Not in winter anyway, on a windy deck. Do you think I have enough gowns? I imagine the Schroeders will do a great deal of visiting.'

The maid suppressed a smile. With two gowns and a costume for 'Sunday best', she considered herself the possessor of a pleasing and generous wardrobe, adequate for all occasions. 'If you are desperate, Miss Faye, I'm sure Mr Schroeder's sister will be able to recommend a good dressmaker.' Frowning, she held up a black dress, simple and modest in shape, which could be brightened by accessories.

Faye shuddered. 'Put it away, Simmy. I hope I'll not have reason to see *that* gown again on this voyage.'

Simmy shrugged. A mourning dress had to be included by all travellers of good taste and sensitivity. Families were large and if one were a guest in a house for some time, like as not some elderly relation of one's host, or perhaps an infant of tender years, would sicken suddenly and die. Out of respect the guests were expected to go into mourning. Socially exalted travellers also had to envisage the possibility of a death in the vast regions of the Royal Family.

Simson turned her attention to the trunks containing accessories. Gloves, shoes, stockings, parasols, fans and feather boas. Undergarments—camisoles, petticoats and lacy drawers which she had sewn for her mistress. A labour of love indeed, to be superseded only by putting the final touches upon Miss Faye's trousseau, which every devoted lady's maid regarded as the grand achievement.

'Aye, miss. You'll definitely be needing more hangers—and more space. Shall I ask—'

'Later, Simmy,' Faye interposed hastily. 'You've done enough and you must be weary. Take a rest—here, on the sofa, and perhaps you'd like to read the messages.' She indicated a stack of *Bon Voyage* cards which lay beside the flowers. As Simmy read them to her, Faye blinked back tears. Their loving messages made her lonelier than ever.

'Such dear, kind friends—and so thoughtful. I shall write thank you notes immediately, so that they can be mailed from Cherbourg.'

'This one is from Lady Mary—'

'Oh, then they are back from honeymoon?'

'There is a letter with it, miss.'

'I shall read that one later, Simmy.' Lady Mary was her dearest friend who had married a distant Wainwright cousin, due to some match-making on Faye's part. When she discovered that cousin David was attracted to her pretty friend she made sure he had ample invitations to visit from his home in Yorkshire.

As Simmy read the next card, she realised that no one would ever guess Faye's secret—that her porcelain beauty was flawed. The word was Faye's, not her own, for she thought her young mistress perfect in every detail.

· But Faye was chronically short-sighted and she refused to wear spectacles, even in Simmy's presence. Over the years with her maid's help she had managed to conceal this disability in public. Simmy was very skilful at interpreting her mistress's needs and averting dangerous situations which threatened embarrassment or disaster. But Simmy had a new worry. She decided that this ship with all those stairs and steps was going to be a constant nightmare if Faye refused to wear spectacles.

Sir Joshua was quite unable, man-like, to understand such a fuss over female vanity, but Faye protested that they were so ugly and she felt humiliated having to wear them. As for the lorgnette, which was her grandfather's cheerful alternative, she uttered a scream of horror. Only dowagers and quite old ladies resorted to such aids. He would be advising an ear trumpet next! Sir Joshua's laugh had been unsympathetic and Simmy wondered if the real reason was that Faye feared it might scare the young gentlemen away, if she didn't have the evidence of her own eyes.

She had long since observed that her mistress's condition was not altogether a disadvantage. Her slight hesitations and uncertainties and that slightly intense expression gave her an air of vulnerability, of mystery and tenderness which drew the young gentlemen like bees to honey—or was it more like knights to a damsel in distress, thought Simmy, smiling to herself.

The lass had a nature as beautiful as her face, which was not always the case these days. Besides, had she been ugly as sin, the Wainwright fortune was enough enticement for the trail of suitors who had made their way to the great mansion since Faye's 'coming-out'.

While Faye read her friend's letter, Simmy returned to the urgent matter of closet space.

'I'm thinking it's the Captain we'll need to talk to, miss, for an extra cupboard or two.'

Faye gathered the messages together. 'What do you think of him, Simmy?'

And Simmy, who in her dour Scots fashion never made snap judgments about anything or anyone, pursed her lips. 'He's a real Celt, I'm thinking.' she said at last, with a sniff of disapproval.

'Oh, is that why he's so—well, foreign-looking?'

'It is. That black hair and eyes, there's plenty with that colouring among the folk from the Western Isles. Some say it's a throwback to the days when the Spaniards from the Armada were shipwrecked as they fled from the English ships.' Simmy shook her head. 'But I've heard tell that it goes a lot further back than that—way back to when the fairy folk ruled the land. That would account for the Celts being gey strange—they're a different race, ye ken, to us Glasgow Scots. Terrible wild and cruel they were in days gone by,' she added with a shocked whisper.

'What did they do?'

'Murdered each other, and worse, not fit for your young ears, miss.'

Faye smiled. Did Simmy not know that every school-child learnt England's early history had also been a blood-bath?

'But they do know more about magic than ordinary mortals,' Simmy admitted grudgingly. 'They have the "second sight", and some even have the gift of pro-phecy. Heathen folk, they are, the lot of them, and not answerable to any man's laws.'

'It all sounds very romantic,' said Faye.

'Romantic!' Simmy's eyes rolled heavenward. 'Romantic, is it? Well, I wouldn't want to meet up with one of them on a dark night, that I wouldn't.'

'I dare say we have nothing to fear from Captain MacManus,' said Faye with a giggle, 'on a dark night or otherwise.'

'I expect he knows his place,' sniffed Simmy.

Faye smiled. Simmy made the formidable Captain sound like a wild animal, carefully domesticated, but whose temper was still treacherous and uncertain.

'He's very handsome, don't you think?'

'Handsome is as handsome does, miss,' said Simmy enigmatically and closed her lips firmly upon the subject, while Faye decided secretly that those looks fitted per-fectly the legend of his ancient race.

There was absolutely no humility about the Captain. He might be her grandfather's employee but she knew instinctively that his proud spirit called no man master. She suspected that his pride would be unshakeable and wished suddenly that he had been a comfortable ordin-ary Scot like Simmy, who was large, sandy and whole-some. She frequently reminded Faye of a friendly lion-ess.

The Scots Faye knew from points south and east of the Hebrides had titles and spent most of their year in comfortable London mansions, returning to their draughty inhospitable Scottish castles as little as poss-ible. A few weeks in autumn was considered quite long enough to mow down large quantities of birds and deer, or to entertain Their Majesties when they were in residence at Balmoral Castle.

Suddenly Simmy, who was sensitive to any movement on water, exclaimed: 'Oh miss, I believe we're under way.'

Faye could hear the throb of engines. 'We must go on deck—quickly.' And pausing only while Simmy slipped her coat across her shoulders, she ran to the door. Simmy steered the way, through corridors and along steps, careful to indicate by slight pressure on Faye's elbow where the hazards lay.

On deck it was almost dark and from the shore pin-points of light lay like bright eyes watching the ship depart. Rainbow-coloured streamers stretched from ship to shore as all around them the passengers took farewell of their friends.

'God speed—*au 'voir—bon voyage*—'

Faye joined them at the rail, realising that in the blurred mass of faces staring up from the quay, there was not a single loving farewell intended for her.

The light from the Captain's bridge caught her in its beam and Gavin MacManus, who had very sharp eyes, saw her surreptitiously wipe away a tear as the *Atlanta* slowly swung round her great girth and, with the tugs hooting in salute, slid out of harbour.

Darkness had fallen quickly and the sky changed from angry red to deep blue and into black; the wind hummed through masts and rigging and the giant funnels became indistinguishable from the blackness of the night.

Captain MacManus, his ship safely under way, breathed freely for the first time. The beam of light again touched the now empty place by the rail which the Wainwright girl had occupied. Her display of emotion remained obstinately with him. He shook his head. He was used to witnessing tearful farewells. His compassion for this solitary girl was inexplicable as he tried to shrug aside that one forlorn picture indelibly etched in his mind.

He hoped fervently that the girl was a good sailor for there would be troubles ahead with severe weather predicted and all the worries and dangers of a good-going Atlantic gale.

Again his thoughts turned to Faye Wainwright. He decided to be polite and courteous, but he did not intend to put himself or his time at the disposal of Sir Joshua's granddaughter just because she was also the Wainwright heiress. He thought cynically that there would be plenty of male passengers eager to do just that. He had already marked down several known fortune-hunters, habitual passengers who crossed the Atlantic in the sole hope of landing a rich wife. Maybe he should warn the girl—if she was as innocent as she looked.

He was met by the Purser, Mr Ewing, also concerned about the weather. He had heard it was going to be bad—very bad.

'We had better be prepared for a rough crossing,' the Captain admitted. Sixty-six miles away lay their first port of call, Cherbourg, but already as the *Atlanta* moved towards the open sea, the first gales thudded into them.

'Aye, sir. I expect there'll be few with stomachs strong enough to sit through dinner this evening,' said Mr Ewing as he fell into step beside him. 'And those who believe that the Atlantic can't possibly have worse weather up its sleeve will have a surprise in store.' The Purser tended to gloom at the best of times.

'What of steerage? What's it like down there?'

'Now that you ask, Captain, they're all huddled together, for warmth, like as not. Most without even a decent shawl or coat fit for land, let alone sea. Did no one tell them it'll be colder than Britain in Halifax—and in New York? Poor devils.'

'We can't clothe them, only feed and accommodate them, Mr Ewing,' said the Captain reproachfully and the Purser remembered that Sir Joshua's illness had prevented the improvements to accommodation that Captain MacManus had pressed for while he was First Officer.

The Purser sighed. 'At least there'll be no complaints from that quarter, sir, no ringing of bells half the night, wanting the steward's help.'

The Captain nodded, knowing that the emigrants would merely suffer or endure for none would listen much less do anything to ease their lot. They would merely be told to thank God they had a brave new world awaiting them across the Atlantic.

He left the Purser thoughtfully. At least the Wainwright Line let them travel for a mere pittance and gave them good plain nourishing food. Sir Joshua had seen to that. Sometimes the meats supplied were the first their starving children had ever tasted, or would taste again for a long time.

And Gavin MacManus remembered uncomfortably that only a generation, a lot of ambition—and a lot of luck—separated him from the social upheaval wrought by the Highland Clearances on the Isle of Skye, when most of his own clan had emigrated in their hundreds, sailing down the Clyde in coffin ships—their destination the Colonies or the Americas.

He shook his head. He could no more have commanded one of those notorious vessels, than he could have carried manacled slaves in the hold.

Faye was surprised to open the door to Captain MacManus. A completely irrational impulse, of which he had very few—and which he was later to regret—had led him to pay a courtesy call upon his illustrious passenger.

'Is all in order, Miss Wainwright?'

The maid had arranged the flowers and the huge banks of orange, bronze and purple blooms cast the melancholy odour of chrysanthemums upon the room. They seemed to add a strange poignancy and an extra dimension of loneliness to the slender girl with golden hair.

'I am a little short of space, Captain.'

'So I observe,' he said drily.

'Oh no, I don't mean the flowers. They are perfectly lovely—I mean, what I do need are extra closets for my clothes.' His sudden frown, his darting glance intimidated her and she found herself, usually in command of every situation, stumbling out apologies. 'You see, Captain, I am not remaining in New York—I am travelling on to Virginia and as the climate will be milder there, I understand. I need a variety of clothes—'

The Captain hardly listened to her explanations: twenty pieces of luggage were enough to contain the wardrobes, aye, and household effects of an entire consignment of steerage passengers and yet she who had so much, had the effrontery to grumble. No, she wasn't grumbling, she was smiling at him. He sighed, for her smile was almost irresistible. Maybe he could find her a tiny extra closet . . .

'I will see what the steward can do for you, ma'am.'

'Would you really?' The wide-open eyes before him were dazzling in their radiance. 'That is so kind, so very kind of you,' she said softly.

The Captain looked around, searching for something to prolong the conversation. His eye alighted on the photograph of Sir Joshua. He heard himself murmuring platitudes about the old captain's health.

'Yes, he is better again. Much improved indeed. So disappointed not to be making this voyage.'

'I am glad to hear that he has made a good recovery.'

'Indeed yes, he needs only rest, according to the physicians.'

A flicker of astonishment appeared on the Captain's face and was rapidly extinguished. That was not the story Sir Joshua had told him at their last interview.

Faye was staring at the flowers, following what she imagined was his reproachful glance in their direction. 'I suppose there are rather a lot—and there would be more space if we removed some. Perhaps your less fortunate passengers in steerage, might appreciate a cheerful gift—'

'This is not a hospital ship, ma'am,' he said stiffly. Her damned charity infuriated him. 'And our less fortunate passengers, as you call them, have little need of flowers, with less room available to house entire families than your maid has to sleep in—' As he darted a finger in the direction of the extra cabin, he knew that he had gone too far. The maid's face, frozen in astonishment, stared across at him as she unfolded her mistress's garments from their shrouds of tissue paper, the only possible way to keep creases at bay.

'I'm sorry, I apologise,' Faye said, with a sad shake of

her head. 'I expect it is food they require, not flowers.' She smiled. 'They can't eat flowers, can they?'

He swept aside her attempt at reconciliation. 'They get excellent meals on my ship, ma'am, you may be sure of that,' he snapped. 'And I see to it personally.'

'Then take the fruit,' she said wearily. 'Please, for the children, at least. I'm sure they will appreciate a little extra fresh fruit—and it's so good for them.'

Gavin MacManus bit his lip. He had the devil's own temper when it was aroused and this golden girl of Wainwrights succeeded in angering him more than all the hoity-toity dowagers, the countesses and the newly-rich. What on earth was getting into him? He bowed. 'If you'll excuse me, ma'am, I have important matters to attend to. The steward will follow your instructions.'

She smiled, nodding assent, and he observed the hurt puzzlement in her eyes. He was furious with himself and gave vent to his feelings by banging the door—almost, but not quite.

As he returned to his own quarters, he decided there was something very odd indeed about Sir Joshua's granddaughter travelling all the way to Virginia at this time of the year, alone but for her maid.

A terrible thought struck him. Had Sir Joshua appointed her an unofficial spy, to report on his performance as commander of the *Atlanta*? Sir Joshua had spent a fortune—so he heard—on fitting new engines which he hoped would make the *Atlanta* the fastest liner on the Ocean:

'I have to inform you, MacManus, that the sum of one thousand pounds will be yours, if you can shorten our existing run to Halifax by twenty-four hours.'

Those were Sir Joshua's last words as they parted. One thousand pounds. Such a sum was a fortune. With it he could accomplish his own personal dream, turn it from fantasy to workable reality—

He shivered. If he failed to shorten the *Atlanta's* Canada run by one day, after the expense of the new engines, he had a feeling that his own days as her Captain would be numbered.

As for that story about Sir Joshua being in perfect

health and needing only rest—it was nonsense. Hadn't he had it from the old man's lips himself, that he was dangerously perhaps even fatally ill. And yet at such a time, he had sent away his beloved granddaughter.

Aye, there was some mystery about Miss Faye Wainwright that aroused the Captain's curiosity. And Sir Joshua too, usually the most direct and honest of men, seemed to be behaving in a mighty devious manner. For some reason, known only to himself, he had concealed the truth from his granddaughter.

If Sir Joshua's behaviour struck the Captain as odd, it struck Faye with alarm regarding the future.

Her maid, although struggling valiantly to pretend that all was well, was showing ominous signs of *mal de mer*. Faye wondered how on earth she could face the days stretching ahead if Simmy succumbed to seasickness. She would be useless as companion, chaperon or maid.

Faye sat down weakly. What on earth would she do without Simmy or Grandfather's consoling presence, smoothing the way through each day. Why, she had never had to consider more than the choice of gowns, or what jewellery to wear. As for doing her own hair—

And then she remembered that Cherbourg lay ahead. Cherbourg—an oasis, an escape route. When they reached port, she and Simmy could leave the *Atlanta*, take passage on a ship returning to Southampton. The thought was instant bliss.

And then sanity returned. No. She would never dare face Grandfather, for cowardice was the one weakness he did not understand and therefore could never forgive. Letting the side down—letting the family down ran a close second. She had been brought up from her earliest days to regard promises made as sacred duties, and she had given her word that she would go to Virginia.

She looked at his photograph with tearful eyes. 'Oh, why did you make me *promise?*' And worst of all, if only she could shake off this terrible feeling that she might never see him again. Although he insisted that he was feeling quite well, she remembered how yellow and old he looked at their parting. And how sad. He who never betrayed the slightest emotion had clasped her to him again and again, and she had felt a suppressed sob rack his gaunt frame.

She put a hand over her mouth, stifling a cry of terror. The thought of never seeing her beloved grandfather again scared her more than anything the Atlantic Ocean could brew up in the way of storms.

It was as well for Faye's uneasiness that she had been absent from home a few weeks earlier, and had not witnessed the scene which had taken place between Sir Joshua and Warren Schroeder. At her dearest friend Lady Mary's wedding reception in London while Faye danced with His Majesty King Edward who, though elderly, retained an admiring eye for a pretty young filly, her own future was already being decided at Wainwrights.

Warren Schroeder had felt very pleased with himself that day as the white Mercedes, sent by his host, carried him through the vast parkland of Sir Joshua's estate. Fifty years earlier, the original Elizabethan manor house had been torn down and replaced by the 'new' Wainwrights. Sir Joshua's father had, alas, never seen his dream of a large family come to fruition within its Gothic-turreted walls. An only son had in turn produced an only son, Faye's father, who had been killed in a riding accident three months before her birth. The shock had also killed any desire Faye's mother—his bride of less than a year—had to survive childbirth. The role of parenthood descended upon Sir Joshua, and the orphaned girl and the *Atlanta* became the whole of his heartbroken lonely existence.

Even measured by wealthy Virginian standards, Warren's suite in the guest wing was opulent. The windows led on to a balcony which overlooked the park where deer grazed amid ancient oaks. He felt like a king surveying his kingdom that sunny October afternoon, especially when his host added casually:

'These rooms were occupied by King Edward and

Queen Alexandra—when they were Prince and Princess of Wales.'

Warren knew how delighted his sister Dulcie would be with that particular piece of information. He looked at Sir Joshua and observed how much he had aged since their last meeting. Both men knew that luxury and riches were small consolation for the loneliness that could seep through majestic but perpetually empty rooms where the sound of one's own footsteps echoed across floors, whether of common wood or Florentine marble.

Sir Joshua had been a widower for a very long time. Warren's marriage had been childless and for years he had nursed a beloved invalid wife whose courage and sense of humour had kept her interested in the plantation and their racehorse breeding until her death. Warren's world had been shattered by this event, bereft of her encouragement and her cheerful, wise presence.

Yes, he decided, Mavis would have been delighted to know the purpose of his visit, for Sir Joshua wished to sell not only the Wainwright shipping line, but also the almost legendary *Atlanta*.

Normally an unsentimental man, Sir Joshua seemed anxious to recall bygone days as they sat over their port at the end of an excellent dinner.

'Remember our very first meeting in Hamburg, Warren? And almost our last, as I recall. You were buying horses, the first of the Schroeder strain.'

Warren smiled, cradling his glass. 'A sentimental return for me, sir. My father had left in considerable haste—a political refugee—for America, the year before I was born.'

Warren and Sir Joshua had been in a Hamburg dockside inn when the brawl ensued and Sir Joshua's mighty fist had diverted the knife wielded by a drunken sailor. Warren shivered at the memory. He doubted whether he would ever be as close to death again.

'I couldn't move as fast these days,' sighed his host.

'You saved my life, sir, and changed my luck too.'

The racehorses had bred a couple of winners and the tobacco plantation blossomed into prosperity. One day Warren awoke to the happy discovery that he was a millionaire. But alas, his beloved Mavis was paralysed as a result of a riding accident and all his riches couldn't make her walk again.

Climbing the gracious winding staircase to his suite, with the family portraits staring down from the walls, Warren was reminded that the dead Wainwrights far outnumbered the living and that their acumen and brave deeds had been filtered down to one old man and a girl.

Since idle hours ticking away also meant dollars un-accumulated, Warren Schroeder begrudged the necessi-ty of more than a minimum spent in sleep. Long before the clock struck seven, he had already digested the documents concerning Sir Joshua's ownership of the Wainwright Line and his valet was attending to his toilette. In the vast, empty breakfast room, Warren paced the floor, avoiding his reflection, that of a rather stout, short and balding man whose only attribute re-mained a pair of still young and bright dark eyes.

Punctually at the last stroke of eight, Sir Joshua appeared. Helping himself from the sideboard laden with chafing dishes, out of all proportion to the number of breakfasters, he pointed to the papers in Warren's hand.

'You've read them?'

'I have, sir, and I'm afraid that all is far from well.' Warren paused before continuing. 'These financial re-ports are not quite what you led me to expect.' He sighed heavily. 'The truth of the matter is—and I don't know quite how to tell you this—the Wainwright Line is bankrupt.'

'Bankrupt!' Sir Joshua whispered and then he shrug-ged. 'I rather expected something of the sort.'

'Those new engines you've had fitted—'

'It had to be done, Schroeder. The old ones were well beyond the safety requirements—and I wasn't going to risk any of my crew or the passengers.'

'That's all very well, sir, but surely you realise that you've been running the *Atlanta* on prices that are completely unrealistic.'

'I cut my prices two years ago in 1904, when all the lines were indulging in a "cut-rate" war—and I've always kept the fares as low as possible for those poor devils in steerage. I'm very particular about where I make my money, you know,' he added severely. 'Besides the new engines should change all that—they should make the *Atlanta* the fastest Royal mail steamer on the Canada run.'

It was true. And in the next moment Warren could hardly believe his ears, as Sir Joshua asked: 'Would you be willing to buy me out?'

'You don't mean that—seriously?' Warren sounded shocked.

'I do. Not only the Line but this house and estate too. All I need is a settlement for Faye, until such time as she marries.'

Warren's mouth opened and shut. The words failed to come. The ship *and* the house. He had never for a moment imagined such a possibility, not in his wildest dreams. What an investment it would make. And he'd be damned sure he ran it on a profit. His mind raced ahead—

Sir Joshua laid a hand on his arm. 'Old friend, I have another reason,' he said heavily. 'I'm a dying man.' He cut short Warren's protests. 'It's true, they've given me six months at most. If I have an immediate operation, this might be extended to a couple of years.' He waved aside Warren's shocked exclamation of sympathy. 'I'm not unduly concerned for myself. I've had a good innings, but I would like to see the Wainwright Line on its feet again, the *Atlanta* in good hands, and my girl settled down. She recently refused young Haversham, the Earl of Darleigh's son. Good fellow, bit wild, but nothing that marriage won't cure.' He sighed. 'She's far too choosy, says she's not in love, all that sort of nonsense. However, with me out of the way, she might think twice about the virtues of settling down, raising a family, that sort of thing. After all, it's what the good Lord intended for womankind.' He paused, tapping his fingers against the table. 'May I ask you a favour, Schroeder?'

'Anything, sir, just you name it.'

'Is that long-standing invitation to Virginia for Thanksgiving still on the cards?'

'Why, sir, you know the answer to that. As I told you long ago, you are more than welcome. Besides, the climate at this time of year is fairly good—it might help—'

'No. I'm not interested in helping myself to stay alive. I'm ready to cross the bar and set sail for another harbour.' When Warren frowned, he continued: 'The girl? Would she be welcome alone?'

Warren said: 'Of course, sir, of course she would.'

'That's fixed then. I'm both relieved and grateful to you.' He gazed over the parkland. 'I shall go into hospital next month just as soon as the *Atlanta* sails again. Thank God my first officer is reliable. One of those no-nonsense Scotch fellows, a born sailor. Bit young to be promoted to Captain, but sound as a rock, and proud as the very devil into the bargain. If anyone can get the *Atlanta* the record, he can.' Sir Joshua sighed. 'Anyway, I want the girl out of England, in case of any, well, unpleasantness to be faced in the immediate future. If I don't recover, by the time she gets back, it'll be all over and done with. I want her to remember me as I am now, no funerals and that sort of thing.'

Warren thought cynically that this was one particular fact of life that Sir Joshua could not spare his granddaughter for ever. Not even Faye Wainwright could go through life cushioned against that part which was as inevitable as birth. No, sir, it was all part of creation, the divine pattern of existence.

'She is most welcome to come to Virginia, and she may stay as long as she likes. My sister Dulcie will be there, as chaperon, of course,' he added hastily, 'just as soon as she sells the house in Halifax, she'll be coming back to live with me—now that I'm alone.'

'Faye will have Simson with her.' Sir Joshua was a little shocked by the hastiness of his response. He had met Dulcie a couple of times and she was not a type that appealed to him, physically a lustily handsome woman, but flighty—even fast. His impressions had proved right, for Dulcie, who was then married to a wealthy Canadian banker had recently been divorced. The accompanying scandal which neither Warren's fortune nor Dulcie's husband could keep out of the newspaper headlines, had caused a considerable stir on both sides of the Atlantic. It made both Sir Joshua and Warren uncomfortable, for divorce was a social stigma, not lightly to be undertaken, and a matter of delicacy for discussion, even between old friends, especially when it concerned one of the family. Of course, everyone knew that some married couples were unfaithful, especially in high society and Royal palaces, but as long as they were discreet—

When Warren Schroeder left later that day, he was owner of the Wainwright Line, also the fine house and its estates. He blinked several times, like a dreamer who must awake to reality, he could hardly credit his good fortune. He could not wait to tell Dulcie and had already arranged that she would join the *Atlanta* and accompany Faye to Virginia where he would be waiting to welcome them.

Over the whole venture, he had only one regret—he wished the Wainwrights had kept the Elizabethan manor, since Virginia revered antiquity above all things. As for the *Atlanta*, he had already decided, despite Sir Joshua's glowing references, that Captain Gavin Mac-Manus's fate lay in the balance.

Warren Schroeder's own business interests which were on the increase in Halifax, would benefit by a speedier passage of Royal mail between Canada and England.

This was the chance for those new engines—and Captain MacManus—to prove themselves. Schroeder was a man who liked proof positive, and he had learned long ago that most poorer men responded to rewards offered. Let MacManus break the existing record from Southampton to Halifax and he'd not only get one thousand pounds, but also guarantee of a command in the Schroeder Line.

If he failed—well, then, Warren Schroeder was not a man to tolerate failures and he knew of two excellent and well-experienced captains who had served with the Hamburg-Amerika and the Norddeutscher Lines, who would jump at the chance of the salary he would be prepared to pay the commander of the *Atlanta*.

As for Faye Wainwright . . . In the absence of any near kin, he had agreed to take care of her affairs, to act for her as guardian until she married.

'She's going to need a father figure,' said Sir Joshua.

He sighed, recalling their parting. For the two old friends it was highly emotional, despite the air of bravado and the pretence that this was just one other '*au revoir*'. Both men knew in their hearts that they were unlikely ever to meet again.

Warren regarded the parkland thoughtfully as the white Mercedes sped him in the direction of Southampton. He had not seen Faye on this visit, as she had remained in London with friends after the wedding.

He remembered her as a shy schoolgirl, pretty in that pale, highly bred English fashion. When Sir Joshua produced a recent society portrait, Warren was unprepared for the beautiful, poised and elegant young woman, who obviously knew exactly how to dress.

Warren brooded upon that picture. His life sorely lacked one essential which had troubled him over the years. He had everything that money could buy, but he had an idea that Faye Wainwright might be able to provide the one ingredient every ambitious millionaire pined for.

And that ingredient was: class!

CHAPTER
THREE

THE first and most important event of the voyage was life-boat drill. Passengers shyly took stock of each other on the well-illuminated decks and exchanged friendly greetings with those near at hand. Faye would have enjoyed drifting into one of the small groups afterwards but Simmy was exhibiting signs of distress and it was the maid who leaned on her mistress's arm as they made their way back to the stateroom.

Faye recognised symptoms of approaching sea-sickness and was adamant that Simmy lie down immediately. Simmy protested.

'I'm just a wee bit dizzy, miss—and my head's buzzing something awful.'

Faye viewed with some alarm this rapid turn of events. That Simmy should succumb when they were hardly out of sight of land and at the slight motion of the ship which she herself found rather comforting! The *Atlanta* had just reached the Channel. What would happen once they hit the sea—or rather, the North Atlantic Ocean hit them—she did not dare to think.

Beyond the porthole was hazy blackness, a combination of winter night and foam-flecked sea, where the ship's rail seemed to move up—and down—and up again.

Faye shivered. She knew that nervous travellers might have good reason for anxiety. She was under no illusions, and never had been. Grandfather's words came back to her with startling suddenness: 'No other ocean inspires such fear and respect in the men who sail her, for the Atlantic is the most dangerous body of water, the most treacherous in the entire world.'

Her personal memory was quite different. As an eight-year-old sitting on the captain's bridge with grand-

father in his uniform, the deck-officer at his instruction
allowing her to hold the wheel, guiding the great liner
across the ocean. Then she recalled the sunny days of
playing hopscotch on deck to the rhyme the sailors
taught her:

'July, stand by:
August, you must,
September, remember;
October, all over—
Then back to the Winter North Atlantic again.'

She picked up her grandfather's photograph. If only
he were here. She was sure that, Canute-like, he could
quell even the mightiest ocean and urge it to obey him.
Nothing could go wrong, she thought superstitiously, on
his ship, *while he was in command.* All her life she had
been used to having her fears calmed by his soothing
words. She smiled. He had even made the long journey
she was taking alone to Virginia sound like the greatest
adventure.

She looked around her, knowing that many girls
would envy her this voyage, this beautiful room which—
portholes excepted—was impossible to reconcile to a
ship at sea. And at the end of the voyage, a wonderful
holiday in America lay in store. Yet she had to admit she
was lonely, utterly lonely and bereft. Except for Simmy,
she had no one. She frowned at the closed door, for it
didn't look as if she was even going to have much of her
maid's society on this particular voyage.

She listened to the sounds outside. Above the slight
vibration of the engines, she heard laughter, footsteps,
music. Opening the door, the strains of a waltz drifted
towards her.

So they were really under way at last. That delightful
seductive sound meant that the ship's orchestra had
begun to play and with it the life of the ship sprang into
being. Oh, she *must* go on deck—at once!

'Simmy!'

To summon her maid was instinctive. Faye had
reached her door knowing that Simmy would spring into

immediate action, eager to serve, uncomplaining. Uncomplaining, however ill she felt.

No. She couldn't be so heartless. Poor Simmy was fast asleep. And if the weather did worsen, this might be her last chance to rest well for some time.

So Faye decided to let sleeping maids lie! There was no earthly reason, except her short sight, why she should not explore alone. 'And if you wear your spectacles, you will be quite safe,' she told herself.

'Never!'

That was one humiliation she was not prepared to face. She thrust out her chin determinedly, reasoned that if she walked slowly, holding the rail, taking small steps and following closely the other passengers—well, on land such behaviour might seem odd, but here on the liner tonight, everyone would be taking extra care, discovering their 'sea legs'.

She peered at her reflection in the mirror. She did not need Simmy's assistance to change, for the rule was that no one dressed for dinner on the first night out; the grand toilette was saved for later occasions. Besides, the blue velvet travelling costume was pretty and elegant too, since it had come straight from the workroom of Monsieur Worth in Paris just two weeks ago.

All sadness and melancholy vanished and she felt slightly wicked at her own boldness. What an adventure, she thought happily, as she made her way carefully along the corridor, staying close to the walls with their discreet handrails and congratulating herself on the ease with which she found the balcony.

There was absolutely nothing difficult about finding one's way about this ship. The balcony rail was already crowded by other promenaders who, while pretending to applaud the orchestra in the dining-room below, were covertly inspecting their fellow voyagers in the game of 'spot the famous'.

Faye found the atmosphere exciting, and made delightfully romantic by the orchestra playing 'The Merry Widow' waltz, one of her favourite pieces, so appropriate in this beautiful setting.

Her limited range of vision revealed most of the

passers-by as couples who held hands, or walked closely arm-in-arm, so she guessed that a fair number of honey-mooners made up the passenger list.

She sighed and turned away, wondering whether it would ever happen to her, this magic madness of falling in love. Lately Grandfather had hinted that twenty was 'getting on a bit'.

She had after all been presented three years ago shortly after her seventeenth birthday. When Faye pro-tested that she was not the least bit 'in love' with Sir Somebody or Lord Someone's heir, or any of the trail of suitors who came to Wainwrights in search of an heiress, Grandfather declared such things unimportant. Mar-riage, said he, was a business alliance between great families in which property and the succession to a title were settled.

She tried to imagine what people in love felt for each other. Closing her eyes, she swayed to the throbbing notes of the waltz. When it ended, she applauded, smiling vaguely in the direction of her immediate neigh-bours at the rail.

The two young men bowed, returned her smile. The quizzical glances exchanged behind her back were almost a code of procedure, meaning nothing to Faye, had she even observed them. Her own action was spontaneous, an honest rush of goodwill and friendliness which ignored the rigid conventions regard-ing communication with strangers of the male sex, even those of equal social standing.

Again she smiled, without coquetry. This was misin-terpreted by the older man who bowed:

'We have not had the honour of an introduction, ma'am, but I believe my sister had the pleasure of meeting you last season at the Devonshires' place.' There was a pause in which Faye was supposed to say; 'Of course', to this piece of fiction, in the interests of propriety. When she frowned the man before her said: 'Name is Parsons. Friend here is Edgeworth.'

Faye's desperate attempt to get their faces clearly into focus gave her a provocatively dreamy expression. The looks exchanged by the two men spoke worlds. What a piece of luck! An absolute stunner—and alone! No wedding ring.

'I don't recall your sister, sir, but then—' Faye paused, embarrassed. With her affliction, she rarely recalled the faces of anyone unless they were met constantly. She had to rely on her excellent memory for voices. 'Faye—Faye Wainwright,' she said, holding out her hand.

Introductions exchanged, Parsons bowed: 'Perhaps we might be permitted the honour of promenading with you, ma'am.'

'Indeed yes, a capital idea. Capital,' announced Edgeworth.

'*Mr* Parsons!' The voice was female and shrill.

'*Mr* Edgeworth!' The second voice was also female and accusing. 'We have been searching for you—everywhere!'

Two very indignant ladies swam into Faye's line of vision. In common with the gentlemen who addressed her, they had superficial airs of elegance with which their voices were not quite in accordance. That they were exceedingly angry was not left in the slightest doubt, as they bore off Faye's new acquaintances before further introductions could be effected.

'Sorry, m'dear, thought you were resting until dinner,' Mr Parsons' apologetic murmur did not escape Faye's sharp ears.

'Just taking a stroll, y'know, testing the air,' said Edgeworth, whose lady demanded shrilly:

'And who, might one enquire, was that *creature* you were both grinning at?'

The reply was lost as the quartet vanished out of range along the balcony.

Faye sighed. How absurd to make such a fuss and even more absurd to stick by the convention that one must await a formal introduction before exchanging cheery greetings with a fellow-passenger. Her face grew slightly rosy, however, at having been called a 'creature' in a tone that clearly indicated she was classed as a thoroughly undesirable person!

Refusing to allow the unpleasant encounter to dampen her enthusiasm for exploring the ship, she de-

scended the main staircase, brass handrail ever at the
ready.

There were four levels and each landing opened into
an elegant salon. After the first, where all attention was
riveted upon the orchestra, the succeeding salons gave
an impression of quiet grandeur—and emptiness. The
mirrors were arranged cleverly to add an extra dimension and carry magnificence into infinity. The effect was
breath-taking, one of limitless space.

Faye sat down, well-hidden by potted palms and
delicate hot-house plants. With bated breath she took
out her spectacles and the room came sharply into focus.

How absolutely delightful it was. Just like being at
home.

'Yes, ma'am, it is very elegant. The decor has been
copied almost exactly from Sir Joshua's own home.'

The voice belonged to Captain MacManus. Faye
crouched back into the shelter of the palms, praying that
she would escape his notice.

'Really, Captain, how fascinating,' exclaimed a
female voice.

'Many liner owners are more ambitious than Sir
Joshua. There are, I understand, French chateaux and
Jacobean mansions sailing across the Atlantic every day.
And the Wainwrights boast that *their* passengers may
have the additional privilege of seeing nothing at all
that has to do with a ship—not even the sea—if they so
wish.'

As they drew nearer, Faye's hopes that she would be
unnoticed dwindled and she hastily returned her spectacles to her pocket. Although she could no longer see the
Captain clearly, she recognised the female voice as
belonging to the irate woman who had referred to her as
a 'creature'.

'My uncle, Lord Rich, is a great yachtsman and a
personal friend of His Majesty,' the voice continued, 'he
believes that a ship should look like a ship at all times.
And he considers all this furniture and crystal chandeliers and fal-de-rals are a lot of nonsense. If people want
to be on the sea, he says, then they should be prepared to
see it.'

A slight pause, then Faye heard the Captain's cool tones.

'Passengers, ma'am, who travel by the Wainwright Line are frequently gentlemen who desire to reach their destination in a hurry and to enjoy the amenities of the smoking-room in place of their London club. Ladies who travel with them are often troubled by delicate constitutions and wish to remain in their cabins for the entire voyage.'

Faye detected a note of reproach as he added: 'And the *Atlanta* endeavours to give them the service they would expect from a highly efficient floating hotel, without constant disagreeable reminders that they are crossing a great ocean.'

Faye decided that was quite a speech and one of which grandfather would have approved.

'You are not implying, I hope, Captain, that we are in for a rough crossing?' The lady's accusing voice made it apparent that she also believed the Wainwright Line was in full command of the weather.

Captain MacManus evaded the question. 'Your first voyage, ma'am? Then you will find, whatever winds blow outside, there is less vibration on the *Atlanta* than most other liners. The corridor panelling has been heavily insulated with layers of felt which absorb the normal creaking of a ship's timbers. Observe the crystal chandeliers over here, ma'am—let me show you—they are so fixed to remain immovable, regardless of the ship's motion.'

As the Captain continued his reassuring tour, Faye quickly left her hiding-place and continued her cautious descent to the ship's lower levels. She adapted quickly. Stairs would no longer be a hazard now that she recognised their direction of climb was parallel to the fore-and aft-axis of the vessel.

Making certain that she was alone, she donned the hated spectacles which, as if by magic, transformed her surroundings into gilt mirrors, plush sofas and sumptuous carpets. Even the skylights were magnificent: domed glass, bronze-filtered in daylight but by night they would appear as oppressively dark.

She thought of the overheard conversation. The Captain had been well-schooled by her grandfather. Even in summer, the North Atlantic crossing could be notoriously unpredictable. Rare were the days when one sat on deck basking in sunshine. Rich men, impatient financiers and queasy millionaires wished only to cross the treacherous ocean as speedily and safely as possible. Alarms and hazards were dealt with by Captain and crew with inconspicuous efficiency, and their nature kept at all costs from the unsuspecting passengers.

Suddenly Faye realised she was lost. Absorbed in admiration of her surroundings she had become disorientated. She could no longer hear the strains of the orchestra playing. Where on earth was the main staircase?

It was not to be found but there, to the right, was the gold filigree-and-glass elevator. She was saved. It would take her up to the balcony.

With a sigh of relief she stepped inside, closed the door and pressed the top button on the panel. Nothing happened. She tried again—and again—and again. Obviously the wretched elevator was out of action. She pushed the door.

It remained firmly closed against all her attempts to open it. Suddenly she felt the oppressive smallness of the area around her. She might suffocate if she could not get air. Panic rose, a silent scream! She was trapped.

With both fists, she hammered against the glass. 'Help—help me—someone, please—please help!'

Every second she grew weaker, fainter. Dizzy now, too.

At last a voice. 'Keep calm, ma'am. Keep calm.'

'I'm locked in. The door won't open. Please hurry.'

'Listen—listen carefully. There is a lever on your right about three feet from the floor. Got it? Push it to your left.'

As if by magic the door sprang open and Faye found herself staring into the steely gaze of Captain Gavin MacManus.

'Oh, thank you—thank you.' Only the Captain's stern expression prevented Faye throwing herself, sobbing with relief, into his arms. 'I'm afraid I locked myself in, I'm so glad you were passing by—it was awful—awful!'

Captain MacManus sighed. This was just his luck. With all going well on the bridge he was making a final tour of inspection when he heard the commotion in the elevator. For a nightmare moment he thought it had stuck again and his relief was enormous when he discovered it at floor level.

He continued to regard Faye with that unsmiling glance.

He might have known that this silly spoilt lass of Wainwright's would find herself some mischief to get into. He didn't need his Hebridean second sight to tell him that she was going to be trouble. He had known it from the first moment that he clapped eyes on her, and groaning inwardly he decided that the pattern was set for the entire voyage.

He would try to be patient. 'Look —here, where it says clearly: "To open—move to the left".' He sighed wearily. 'It has an automatic locking device for safety once the door is closed.'

Faye stared at the lever. 'I'm sorry. I'm afraid I panicked. I suffer from claustrophobia.' She was shivering. Her fears were genuine and the Captain, looking down on that golden head, resisted an almost overwhelming temptation to steady her with a strong arm about her slim shoulders. He remembered her nearness as a devastating experience sent from Satan himself.

'If there is something more you wish to see on this deck?' His voice was sterner than he intended.

'No. Nothing. I should like to return to my cabin if you will be so good as to direct me.'

At last he smiled. 'Then permit me to accompany you,' he said and opened the door to the elevator. 'Step inside.'

Faye regarded the interior doubtfully. 'Are you sure?'

'You will be quite safe with me.'

The elevator seemed small indeed for two people when he followed her inside and closed the door. Conscious of physical proximity, of arms touching lightly and of her head all but resting on his shoulder, she avoided meeting his eyes reflected on the pink mirror glass of the door.

She discovered that the softer light did much for the Captain's stern countenance. It made him look younger and sculpted those harsh facial angles of cheekbone and chin into quite a different appearance. How handsome he could be, thought Faye, if only he would learn to exercise that slow attractive smile more often!

The elevator gave a sudden jolt and she grasped his arm anxiously.

'Merely a pause at each floor, Miss Wainwright. No need for panic, we'll have you safely back in your cabin directly.' he added soothingly, as though she were a small scared child.

Faye's heart began to beat rapidly. What if this silly elevator broke down and she was imprisoned with Captain MacManus, so close they were practically in each other's arms. The thought made her giggle. A delightful and rather wicked thought—he might even try to kiss her! How awful!

She saw his withering glance in the mirror. Obviously he was untroubled by thoughts of a similar nature. However, his close proximity was very nice indeed.

'There isn't much room, Captain, was it specially designed with sardines in mind?'

Captain MacManus frowned at his reflection, not wishing to remind her that the design had been approved of by Sir Joshua himself. He did not let his mind dwell upon its nasty bouts of temperament and said: 'It is meant to carry two persons.'

He sounded reproachful and Faye gave him an uneasy glance. Did he think that his nearness was offensive to her? As if by mutual consent, they endeavoured to move as far away from each other as space permitted.

As the Captain had promised, the ascent took only one minute. To Faye it seemed much longer, but not altogether an unpleasant experience. In fact, she was rather sorry when it was over. She felt safe with the Captain by her side. If only she could find suitable conversation. Why did this wretched man have the power to intimidate her, solemnly twisting her attempts to be friendly and resisting all her efforts to 'put him at his ease' as Grandfather would have wished?

At last they set foot on the balcony and Faye sighed with relief. 'Thank you, Captain. It was good of you to come to my rescue,' she added with a shy smile.

He bowed. 'It was fortunate I was in the area at the time. Now, if you'll follow me.'

'I know my own way from here, Captain. Thank you.'

But as if she had not spoken, he took her arm firmly and ushered her in the direction of her stateroom. She felt like a truant schoolgirl being marched back to the classroom and was not in the least grateful. Did the Captain regard her as precious cargo, not to be mislaid under any circumstances? It would never do for the lordly commander of the *Atlanta* to have to confess to having mislaid Sir Joshua's granddaughter *en voyage*!

They reached the door in silence, where he bowed again. 'In future, if you wish to inspect the ship, perhaps you will let me know and I will appoint someone to accompany you.'

Had he faintly emphasised the word 'inspect'? Faye's smile faded. Did he think she was examining his wretched ship to take back a full report on his efficiency to his employer? The thought of such an idea having entered his head and motivating his behaviour towards her made her blush.

The door opened, he looked inside: 'Your maid?'

Mercy, thought Faye, now both amused and angry. He wants to hand me over into safe-keeping. He *does* regard me as a piece of cargo!

'I left her asleep. A little under the weather, I'm afraid. Alas, Simson is not a good sailor.'

The Captain's frown deepened. 'I think I ought to warn you that we are in for a bad crossing.'

'I am fully aware of the weather conditions to be expected on winter voyages, Captain.'

He frowned again, his curt nod acknowledging her words.

'We are expecting gale force winds. But you need have no fear, nor your maid, Miss Wainwright. I guarantee that the *Atlanta* will get you to Halifax safely. We are fully in command of the situation and the ship is secure as a rock.'

Faye smiled wryly and faced him squarely. 'You don't have to pretend to me, Captain. I am fully aware that the hazards we might meet, even during the most benign of summers, defy invention. My Grandfather told me that at any time, they read like a seasonal catalogue from—er—'

'Hell, Miss Wainwright,' he supplied. 'From hell. That is correct.' He sighed. 'And as you obviously know, no amount of gilt, marble or plush can conceal the ancient immemorial risks of the sea. And no amount of power from new engines or weight of steel can possibly bring a ship—any ship, even the *Atlanta*—into scale with the Atlantic Ocean.'

This lyrical account of possible dangers seemed to please him for he smiled. 'Besides, a few more thousand tons sailing upon its surface does not intimidate it in the least.'

If he expected Faye to cower in terror, then he was disappointed. She had heard almost exactly these words spoken by Sir Joshua. When she did not reply, he said apologetically:

'You did ask me not to pretend with you.'

Faye straightened her shoulders. 'Are you suggesting, Captain, that I should be afraid?'

He looked at her steadily for a moment, took in the face like a Botticelli angel with its crown of glorious golden hair, the slim beautiful body, the dainty hands and feet. He shook his head. 'I don't think, Miss Wainwright, that you would ever be afraid of anything.' And with the briefest of salutes, he turned on his heel and left her still staring after him.

'Not anything, Captain,' she murmured to herself, 'not anything, but *anyone*!'

Already she was afraid to admit her reactions to the remarkable Captain MacManus. As she closed the door she decided that this discovery was not an unpleasant feeling. Tantalising perhaps, but not absolutely scary—yet!

CHAPTER
FOUR

THE *Atlanta* had docked at Cherbourg to take on new
passengers. Now that the ship was motionless, Faye
once again had Simmy's services. The maid, however,
firmly declined any suggestion that dinner should be
brought to her cabin. Eventually Faye persuaded her to
take a little gruel and warm milk.

Because of her stubborn refusal to see the world
clearly and steadily through the most expensive gold-
rimmed spectacles that money could buy, Faye was
relieved to be having an escort down to the dining-room.
She was at her most vulnerable in crowded places, but
her feelings were very mixed as she awaited the Captain.
In her grandfather's absence it was his duty to take her to
dinner. If only his presence did not undermine her
composure so disastrously.

At last, there was a knock on the door which Simmy
opened to Purser Ewing.

'The Captain's apologies, ma'am, he will be unable to
dine with the passengers this evening.' The Purser did
not expand on what was obvious. The ship was making
very heavy weather and, as most of them had observed,
the last few hours between Southampton and Cherbourg, had been an extremely uncomfortable and ominous prelude. If Faye felt grateful for anything, it was
that the heavy weather outside would not be accompanied by the heavy weather of making conversation with
the enigmatic Captain.

As she descended the grand staircase on the Purser's
arm, the orchestra's selection from Franz Lehar was
being performed to a profusion of potted palms and an
almost empty dining-room. At close quarters, Faye was
aware just how few diners there were.

As the Purser seated Faye at the Captain's table, he

apologised once more for his absence. Glances were
exchanged and a murmur of disapproval came from
among the other guests. Those who had sailed on earlier
voyages of the *Atlanta* knew that it was almost unheard
of for Sir Joshua Wainwright to fail to put in an appearance on the first night out. His large presence was
necessary to console, soothe and answer innumerable
questions.

Studying the menu, Faye decided upon prudence and
ordered a little turtle soup, and duck à la Montmorency,
accompanied by roast potatoes, green peas and an excellent winter salad. Choice of wine was the gentlemen's
province and sipping a glass of white Moselle she decided against any of the exotic desserts which were on
display.

Despite Purser Ewing's valiant attempts to make
everyone feel at ease, Faye was aware of that hollowness
of the heart when one is quite alone and everyone else
appears to have a devoted and amiable companion.

The Captain's table was composed of a pair of honey-
mooners, a French count and countess and the heir
to a Balkan throne who spoke little English and whose
wife devoted herself entirely to the business of eating. The only 'single' person besides Faye was an
elderly lady on the Purser's other side. As she was
rather deaf and misheard every statement, Mr Ewing's
attention was held by her imperious commands throughout the meal.

The dessert had been reached and Faye decided this
was a good opportunity to excuse herself and retire to the
stateroom. She was fatigued with the long day's activity
and dinner threatened to be a wearisome ritual stretching out into two hours. How pleasant to escape the
cheese, coffee, liqueurs and sweet biscuits with which it
would eventually end! She was framing the words to
attract the Purser's attention and make her escape when
she heard her name spoken:

'Faye! Why, Faye old girl, is it really you? What a
surprise. My dear, how absolutely capital to find you
here!'

The voice was familiar and turning she looked into the

handsome countenance, the bright blue eyes and crisply curling hair of the Hon Edward Haversham.

'Teddy,' she exclaimed, 'how lovely to see you!'

'Teddy' Haversham bowed over her hand. 'Just come aboard. Hope I'm not too late for dinner.' He leaned over and kissed her cheek, as he waited for a place to be provided for him.

Purser Ewing rose immediately. 'Please sit here, sir.'

The waiter summoned and the purser's vacant place reset, interest rekindled as the Hon Edward was introduced to the other guests. The younger son of the Earl of Darleigh, his name was constantly in the news, his exploits reported in the society columns—a friend of the King, no less, and a constant escort to many ladies of the Royal circle.

Faye's feelings were rather mixed. Of course, it was delightful and quite unexpected to see Teddy again, and a joy in her present mood to see a familiar face. Teddy did not waste much time, either. Under cover of the pristine tablecloth, he surreptitiously squeezed her hand and whispered in her ear:

'What a stroke of luck, my dear. We shall have such fun.' The determined pressure of his knee against her leg, and his jocular comments about finding her all alone at last, plainly indicated that he had forgotten their last meeting when Faye had slapped his face very briskly. This gesture was in return for his very determined 'pass' during their weekend at a country house which had included trying to force his attentions on her, while very drunk, with an assault upon her locked bedroom door.

'What *are* you doing here?' she asked.

Teddy put down his soup spoon and regarded her solemnly. 'Wired the ship and found they still had a place, so I came aboard just now from Cherbourg.' He shrugged elegant Savile Row clad shoulders. 'The boar-hunting at Weisbester's place was depressingly poor this season, in fact the biggest boar was the Count himself. Mercy it was that no one got the idea of putting *his* head on the vacant platter. Wouldn't even need stuffing—'

And Faye found herself, as always, chuckling at his wickedly amusing and malicious gossip.

'The Pater,' he continued, referring to his father, the Earl, 'has just bought shares in a copper mine in Arizona. Thought it was a good idea that I should go out there and seek my fortune. There are no wars left to fight and the church just isn't for yours truly. Can you imagine me in a surplice armed with holy sentiments?'

Faye had to admit that imagination would not stretch to this almost inevitable disposing of younger sons who had no titles to inherit.

'Well then, what else is a chap to do these days but "go west, young man". Wasn't awfully keen on leaving old England's green and pleasant land, mind you. However, had a run of bad luck at Monte, the devil's own cursed luck, I might add, for the cards were stacked against me from beginning to end.' He paused for breath and then added, 'So—it seemed like a good idea to establish a prudent distance between myself and the Pater till his blood cooled down a little.'

His rueful grin told Faye the rest. Teddy was a notorious gambler, used to playing for very high stakes in the Royal circle. If his losses had been enough to arouse his father's wrath then they must have been considerable. The Earl was well-known to possess a temper to match his ferocious appearance and was not above taking the horse whip to anyone who offended him—and that included his sons.

'But I'm amazed to see you here, Faye, my child. Where on earth are you heading? And where's the Gaffer tonight?'

Faye told him about Sir Joshua's illness, which Teddy decided was no bad thing from his personal point of view. As he listened to the tale of woe, he was delighted to discover that Faye was without the encumbrance of her formidable grandparent. Sir Joshua, alas, seemed to have the ability to read a chap's mind and intentions before the thoughts had even crossed a chap's own mind. Sharp he was, very sharp! He allowed his hand to stray to Faye's knee and was rebuked by her withdrawal, and a look of annoyance. He told himself he must take it easy, and not rush his fences. By heaven, the girl was delectable. Finding her alone like this was a tremendous stroke of luck, and unlikely ever to be repeated.

Teddy had realised, as had most other eligible society bachelors, that the Wainwright fortune was a splendid asset calculated, in his own case, to soothe the Pater's anger in a most extraordinary manner. However, the only way to get at it would be to marry Faye, the apple of her grandfather's eye. Teddy was nothing if not a determined wooer, and if he could persuade her that she was in love with him, then the Gaffer would give his little darling anything her heart desired, including a husband he did not approve of one hundred per cent, or even consider absolutely genuine. However, Teddy was very attracted by Faye and could easily be persuaded that he was in love with her. Even though the Wainwright fortune was tempting, he told himself, he wouldn't be marrying her just for her money.

'Sorry about the Gaffer, Faye old girl. Splendid chap. Who's he put in charge of the boat?'

Faye smiled. Teddy was incorrigible. How poor Grandfather would have winced at the profanity of hearing his divine *Atlanta* referred to as a boat!

'Captain MacManus is in command. Grandfather thinks very highly of him. He was his First Officer—*very* reliable!'

Teddy whistled. 'Must be a paragon then. I'm surprised that the Gaffer found anyone worthy of this magnificent pile.' He looked around the softly-lit dining-room with its panelling, its palms and the discreet orchestra which had now struck up a Strauss waltz. 'All the comforts of home, eh? I'd have imagined that not even Noah leaving the Ark with a fistful of references would have been good enough for the lovely *Atlanta*. What's the good Captain like? Old as Methusaleh and twice as crafty? Beard down to here?' he added, indicating his waist.

Faye chuckled. 'Not in the least. He's quite young for a Captain. In fact—' Her voice faded. 'Here he is now,' she added in a whisper as the Captain stood at the next table. Fortunately he had not heard Teddy's remarks as he greeted the diners, shaking hands with the men, bowing over the ladies' hands, full of profuse apologies for his unavoidably late arrival. 'Unforeseen customs difficulties to sort out— Delays? Yes, indeed but we will soon be under way again.'

Now that he was suddenly in focus, she could see that he was smiling. She gasped, for the effect was charming—more than charming, in fact, it was devastating. There he was, actually throwing back his head with mirth and exchanging some merry quip with one of the ladies. She blinked. Could this disarming, friendly fellow be the same dour Captain MacManus, reserved and prickly, from the outlandish Hebridean Isles?

And now it was her turn.

'Miss Wainwright.' He bowed, lingering over her hand. 'My sincerest apologies for not escorting you into dinner.' And as he was introduced to Teddy, he smiled. 'My loss, I see, was Mr Haversham's gain.'

Good heavens, thought Faye, whatever next? Was he being arch and flirtatious too? His black eyes sparkled with merriment. His voice, which she had thought of as harsh and commanding, was velvet-soft and warm.

'I trust you have all dined well? If you have any complaints, I am sure Mr Ewing will lend a sympathetic ear. He is a very good listener, or so I am told,' he added, putting a friendly hand on the Purser's shoulder.

Another chuckle and he was bidding them goodnight, hoping they would all sleep well. Faye watched his departure wide-eyed. Carrying his cap under his arm, he looked younger, and distinctly more human. His black hair was straight and heavy, with a tendency to fall across his brow in a boyish manner. His lithe figure suggested the athletic field rather than the bridge of a great liner.

He was out of range. Where had he gone, she wondered? Back to his cabin—what would it be like? Severe and leathery? Grandfather's luxuries for his passengers, his concern for their comfort, did not extend to the spartan condition of his own quarters. Or had Captain MacManus gone back to his lonely bridge? She wondered what thoughts filled his head in those long hours staring out over the wild sea.

She was glad when Teddy, who ate with businesslike

speed, finally decided that the meal had reached its end. As he escorted her back to her cabin, she heard the distant purring throb of the engines coming alive. The *Atlanta* was on the move again and all the insulation in the world would never be able to disguise that they had just hit the open sea.

She had a moment's regret about the large helping of Gâteau Napolitan with its heavy coating of marzipan, cherries and cream which Teddy had insisted she eat 'just to keep him company'. That extra liqueur too, on top of the wine! Her knees were decidedly wobbly and she was glad of his steadying arm. She resolved that in future when they dined together she would restrict her intake of alcoholic beverages to a single glass of white wine. Otherwise, those hated spectacles would be needed—

What Faye failed to realise was that Teddy already knew her secret and his guidance was extra careful as well as discreet. He, of all her suitors, had learned long ago that she was short-sighted. His sister Amelia had the same affliction and had told him how, at a houseparty, the two girls had confessed in a singular burst of confidence how truly dreadful it was to have to wear spectacles. Amelia, who was practical and plain, had decided long since in favour of the lorgnette and her disability had not stopped her being courted by a wealthy but—as Faye had observed at the wedding—elderly and unattractive baronet.

Teddy lingered at the stateroom door longer than etiquette dictated. He was remarkably pleased with the evening's events. He felt that he had reinstated himself with Faye and dropped a gentle hint that, as the night was still young, she might like to accompany him to the liner's restaurant for some refreshments before retiring.

His hopes were dashed when Faye shook her head. 'You must excuse me, Teddy. It has been a particularly long and exhausting day and quite honestly, I can hardly keep my eyes open,' she added.

'You look as fresh as a daisy,' said Teddy reproachfully.

'Well, I'm not.' And she failed to suppress a delight-

fully convincing yawn. 'Oh, I do beg your pardon.' She
followed this gesture with a careful evasion of his goodnight kiss and received this comradely salutation—much
to Teddy's chagrin—in the region of her ear, rather than
on her mouth which had been his target.

In the stateroom, Simson, revived by the ship's lack of
motion in Cherbourg, had made a gallant attempt to sort
out her young mistress's overburdened wardrobe.

'They always say, Miss Faye, that the Channel crossing is the worst. If you survive that, then you'll find the
rest is easy,' she said cheerfully. But the ship's movement was already showing in her face. 'No, miss, I'll not
retire, not until I see you settled for the night.'

As the maid helped her prepare for bed, Faye felt it
was tactful to ignore both the ship's increasing motion
and Simmy's rapidly paling face. Surprisingly, she slept
immediately and when she awoke some hours later, it
was to wonder what she was doing in the guest bedroom
at Wainwrights, and what on earth was making the walls
move and creak. The bed too, swayed. Realisation
brought delight—she was at sea on the *Atlanta* and they
were really under way at last. She lay back, hands
clasped behind her head, enjoying the gentle rocking
motion of the ship which she found so soothing.

Through the porthole a great globe of orange arose
from a purple horizon. Sunrise on the sea—how beautiful! There was not a moment to be lost! Suddenly she felt
stifled for lack of air. Dare she go out alone? Perhaps
Simmy was awake—she tiptoed into the little room and
smiled at the recumbent figure. Simmy slept, no doubt
due to the draught which she had brought along 'in case
of emergencies'.

Very well, she could attend to her morning toilette
without assistance. As she donned tweed skirt, shirt
blouse and jacket, she felt exhilarated at this unexpected
self-reliance. It brought the thrill of added adventure,
away from her daily life at home with every move
cosseted and supervised by Simmy.

She pinned her hair rather inexpertly and topped it
with a sensible hat, anchored by hat pins. She wasn't
perfectly satisfied with the final result—Simmy would

never have allowed those tendrils of hair which persisted in descending from under the hat's brim. However, the unequal battle with an army of hairpins bored her and she consoled herself that few other passengers would be promenading this early.

As she added her fur coat to her ensemble, she found herself clutching the back of a chair for support. The portholes were now misted with sea spray and she could hear the steady boom of the sea against the ship's hull as the *Atlanta* bucked like a frightened mare against a heavy sea.

She made her way on deck without difficulty and the clear air struck her as forcibly as heady wine. How intoxicating to inhale the purity of this boundless infinity of a deserted seascape! She breathed deeply and contentedly.

While Faye had the promenade deck to herself, the sky paled into incandescent light and then darkened into the ominous grey of an approaching storm. From the galley there now issued sounds of banging crockery and appetising smells of breakfast in preparation. Most first-class passengers ate this meal in the privacy of their staterooms and made their daily debut in leisurely fashion for luncheon.

She decided to miss breakfast, for she had little appetite for the mammoth meal of kippers from Scotland, bacon from Ireland, English beefsteaks and kidneys— besides the indulgences for weaker stomachs, namely, eggs and porridge. Huge breakfasts had been made fashionable by His Majesty the King and were slavishly followed in high society. They were not for her. After an invigorating walk along the deck, however, she would doubtless be ready to do full justice to luncheon.

As the *Atlanta* gave a sudden unexpected lurch, Faye seized hold of the rail. While she regained her balance, she became aware of being watched.

From the bridge a uniformed figure was surveying the deck. She raised a hand in greeting and thought she received in return a salute, a bow. She smiled, rather proud of herself since only the uniform revealed that the watcher *might* be Captain MacManus—the uniform and some strange intuition which warned her of his presence.

It was indeed the Captain who was both astonished and rather horrified to see Faye Wainwright wandering about the deck at this hour of the morning, without her maid and in such fierce weather. She must be mad, he thought, torn between admiration and irritation at such foolhardy behaviour. He experienced an almost irresistible desire to rush down the steps and escort her safely back to her cabin, while solemnly lecturing her upon the dangers of such outlandish behaviour.

Before the impulse could be put into action, he saw to his relief that she had vanished. Thank heaven the rail was too high for any passenger to fall overboard. Ridiculous thought! Captains were well-advised against being over-imaginative; there were plenty of real-life terrors without the fanciful. As for Faye Wainwright, there were others on board equally as important and he couldn't spend his time playing nursemaid to this spoilt miss, who exasperated him.

The *Atlanta* bucked savagely as a particularly large wave hit her amidships. The Captain groaned. He had troubles enough in store without capricious females and he would be fortunate indeed to get the *Atlanta* to Halifax in safety, much less break any speed record and earn that handsome bounty of one thousand pounds.

At his command to the duty-officer at the wheel, the massive bulk of the ship changed direction in an attempt to evade the full force of the approaching storm.

Captain MacManus stared at the darkening sky overhead and thought of his island home in the far-distant Hebrides. Whatever happened, he had no regrets, even if the cards had fallen in his direction instead of being stacked against him since his birth, he would still have made the same choice.

A green sea swirled biliously across the deck, indicating that it was going to be very rough below for the passengers. Even the *Atlanta's* vast girth would shake about like a floating log before the next twenty-four hours were over. Grimly, the Captain issued instructions that all passengers were to expect heavy seas and that promenade decks were out-of-bounds until they reached calmer weather.

And that, he told himself, should keep Miss Faye Wainwright in *her* place!

CHAPTER
FIVE

Two days out in the Atlantic and Faye felt stifled by the life around her, despite its luxury. Remaining below decks was no real hardship in first-class; in point of fact, some passengers never set foot on deck in winter, and every consideration was given to their comfort and entertainment. The whole voyage was planned around the illusion that they were still on land.

There were other passengers who shared Faye's views. A few who believed that rough weather was precisely what the *Atlanta* was built to withstand and that those much-advertised new engines could deal with anything, even the worst storm that the ocean could bring forth.

And so, in the grand salon each morning at eleven, those fortunate passengers who had gained their sea legs were promenading to the gentle strains of the ship's orchestra. They chose to ignore the sea spray on the windows which hid the turbulent waves and also the occasional violent lurch given by the *Atlanta*. This usually upset coffee cups and often hurled the unsteady into chairs, or had them seizing the nearest rope. Such mishaps were not taken seriously, but greeted with gales of laughter. There was never any real thought of danger from the squalls outside, from which the normally well-behaved *Atlanta* was now taking a severe punishment.

In the comfortable below-deck world, everything ran smoothly and to a strict routine. Coffee and refreshments were served according to the time-table and all meals maintained their excellent and elaborate standards, guaranteed to tempt all but the most unhappy taste-buds.

Tablecloths, however, were dampened by the stewards before each meal to keep the dishes from sliding

and the table edges were raised against further calami-
ties, like soup plates depositing their contents into ex-
pensively-clad laps. Ropes had been carefully stretched
across all open spaces to enable passengers to grab
support when the liner hit a particularly stubborn wave.
All these safety precautions were discreetly noted, but
not dwelt upon at length.

The Winter Garden was Faye's favourite area. It
brought the illusion of being back home in the conservatory of Wainwrights, where she normally spent a considerable part of her free time chatting to the gardeners
about rare plants that flourished under their care.

Here on the *Atlanta*, as the ship ploughed grimly
through mountainous seas, exotic birds called and sang
from high branches and among the spiked blades of
tropical plants, fountains played. One wall was occupied
by an aquarium of rainbow-coloured fishes, swimming in
a miniature ocean bed of fronds and stones. Creepers
hung from marble arches reaching to the sky—even if
that sky was made of blue glass! This pleasant, peaceful
place was as far from the sea as anyone could imagine
and all day long, from dawn to dusk, the birds darted,
whistled and sang.

Faye took with her a novel whose pages she rarely
opened, for she was never solitary for long. Teddy
Haversham had discovered her retreat and now
appointed himself her constant companion. Often she
would rather have been alone, but at other times she was
honest enough to be glad of his company. She had not
fully realised until the voyage was well under way, how
disastrously lonely she might have been had not Teddy
boarded at Cherbourg.

Everyone it seemed had someone, to walk with, to
read with, to share the soft lights of a secluded table in
the Palm Court. Families who travelled were united and
showed no inclination to exchange introductions or stray
beyond their own intimate circle.

'Happy?' asked Teddy, squeezing her hand.

Yes, she was happy enough. Glad too, of Teddy's
amusing company. But she felt it would not last long for
she frequently detected a lingering look which suggested

he had plans to transform their pleasant, easy comradeship into a more emotional relationship.

There was no escape inside. Faye noted that, substituting for a brisk stroll on deck, oxygen was pumped into the public rooms each morning, taking away stale tobacco and food fumes..The other modern marvel was that as darkness descended each day, electric lights went on as if by magic and turned the *Atlanta* into a shaft of bright lights speeding through the night.

'Just think,' said Teddy, 'only a few years ago and passengers were forced to stay in their cabins, lit only by a single oil-lamp swinging above their heads from a hook in the ceiling.' He shuddered. 'Enough to make the strongest stomach queasy, don't you think?'

With Teddy's assistance, Faye explored the ship. The elevator no longer held any terrors, it was a delightful toy in which she gleefully sped up and down between decks, like an excited child.

And how marvellous to have Teddy's steadying hand always at the ready. If it hadn't been for Teddy, she realised gratefully, she would have had to resort to the hated spectacles, for she soon realised the dangers of indulging her vanity when personal safety was at risk. In such unsettled weather, with the *Atlanta's* constantly unpredictable behaviour, she could, more than once, have met with a serious accident.

Now Teddy had become her perfect vision. Sometimes, she suspected, from a word dropped here and there, that he was fully aware of her affliction. She did not mind for she regarded him as a friend. Friends were those who took their loved ones for better or for worse. Besides, if Teddy did know of her disability, it certainly did not make him any less amorous and she began seriously to wonder if the wearing of spectacles would deter a man who really loved her for herself alone.

During their explorations, Teddy took her down to visit the marble swimming pool, a replica of a Roman bath. Now emptied because of the weather, Teddy regarded it sadly.

'When we're in calmer waters, I shall take a dip every morning. Chases the cobwebs away marvellously.

Perhaps you'll join me,' he added, 'I would love to swim with you.'

Faye blushed and did not reply to his proposal. The idea was really quite outrageous and the rules very strict: certain hours for ladies and for gentlemen where each sex could swim in utmost privacy and decorum. Mixed bathing indeed! Grandfather would be shocked to the core that such a thing could take place upon his ship.

'Now, where shall we go next? What is milady's command?'

'I think I should like an aperitif.'

As they made their way up in the elevator, Faye's thoughts were not with Teddy, but with Captain Mac-Manus. She kept on remembering, with shameful persistence, their experience of sharing this elevator together. How exciting his presence then, how electrifying—while Teddy's arm about her shoulder did not thrill her in the least!

Now that the Hon Edward Haversham was recognised by one and all as Faye Wainwright's 'escort', Purser Ewing also seemed eager to accommodate the likely romance by a discreet rearranging of the seating at the Captain's table, so that the two were always side by side. Faye wondered whether this had been done with the Captain's approval.

She was acutely aware of his presence, seated away to her left, and she longed to attract his attention. However, although he was always polite, he did not try to include her in any conversation. She would have liked to pretend that he was jealous of Teddy, but realised it was more likely relief that the burden of 'escorting' her had been removed from him. Strange to say, that thought— and his indifference—hurt.

She watched him narrowly. How elegant and handsome he looked in dress uniform as he took his place at the table. She felt that she was seeing a new version of Captain MacManus as he smoothly and diplomatically conducted conversations away from the bad weather outside, or any sad note of disasters at sea.

Even Teddy was impressed by the Captain's handling of one guest who regarded the whole voyage with an undertaker's solemnity and wished to retell tales of the old days when ships were 'mere sea-coffins, sinking with all hands'.

'Brilliant seamen have to train themselves to act with social graces,' said Teddy afterwards, his admiration tinged with reluctance. 'Graces for which many of them have not the background or, as I suspect in our good Captain's case, neither disposition nor the aptitude that comes with good breeding. But have you noticed the way the old ladies—and even the not-so-old—eye your Captain as if they would like to gobble him up?' When she didn't reply, he asked: 'Do you think he's all that handsome?'

'I haven't thought about it, Teddy,' Faye lied, 'and I do wish you wouldn't call him *my* Captain.'

'Just a figure of speech, old girl.'

Inevitably the rumour that the *Atlanta's* new engines were all set to break the speed record to Halifax had filtered through to the passengers. It had become the subject of dinner time conversation and of a large number of private bets.

'Alas, *mon capitaine*,' said the Count gloomily, 'if this vile weather continues, then I fear we will be unlikely to reach Halifax on schedule, much less break any record.'

The Captain dismissed this prophecy cheerfully. More than the passengers could possibly know—or guess—hung upon his getting the *Atlanta* to Halifax ahead of schedule. Not only the bounty but his whole future career.

'This liner, sir,' he said, 'should start and arrive at its destination with the same punctuality and reliability as that of a railroad train on land.'

'Impossible,' said the Count.

'Begging your pardon, sir, it is not in the least impossible. In fact, such a performance is well within the realms of our established routine.'

'In a sea like this? You joke!' said Faye.

His eyes turned to her slowly. 'Not at all, Miss Wainwright. But I agree with you about the sea, since among the many agreeable gifts God gave to man, He did not include the magic by which man could tame the sea.'

All attention had turned to Faye as Sir Joshua's

granddaughter, whose opinion might be regarded as the oracle. She felt embarrassed by their scrutiny and by the Captain's gaze, which was cold and reproachful.

The Count eagerly seized upon Faye's innocent exclamation and smiled gratefully in her direction.

'A liner, *mon capitaine,* is after all but a ship and the Atlantic can act like a wrathful God, putting frail mortals like ourselves in our proper places!'

'It is ver' hard for any of us to regard all zis—beauty and comfort—as having anything to do with a *race*—?' The Countess flourished a diamond-clad wrist.

The Captain bowed in her direction. 'That, madame, is exactly what the Wainwright Line most earnestly wishes you, its passengers, to believe. The company's brochure declares that the *Atlanta* is not a mere ship but a floating palace.'

The remark was greeted by polite laughter and Teddy said: 'Reigned over by one monarch, eh, Captain?'

'Indeed, sir. To Sir Joshua Wainwright!' The Captain raised his glass. 'May he soon be sailing with us again.'

As the toast echoed around the table, the conversation turned to the absent owner whose personality was stamped upon everything; from ormulu sconces and pink-shell lamps, to the deep blue carpet, the china and linen, all of which bore the Wainwright crest.

Faye listened to reminiscences from those who had voyaged with her grandfather and observed that Captain MacManus did not join in. He remained silent, withdrawn, and Faye, suddenly embarrassed, wondered if Teddy's remark had been subtly to remind the Captain of his place.

As the evening's entertainment drew to a close, Teddy escorted Faye back to her stateroom. She found his physical demands more difficult to evade than usual. He persisted in hugging and kissing her and refused to let her go, ignoring her protests of weariness.

'You can't disappear yet a while, my darling, and leave poor Teddy on his lonesome.'

'I'm tired, Teddy,' she smiled, her hand on the door.

'But it isn't midnight yet and Cinderella can't go home and leave the Prince before the magic hour has struck.'

His voice was slurred and he was not quite steady. Faye realised just how much he had been drinking, not only wine, but several brandies after dinner.

'Come along, old girl, we can go to my cabin.' He seized her arm firmly. 'Just one drink—a nightcap—make you sleep. C'mon.'

When she struggled, he took her face between his hands and began to kiss her passionately. Indignantly she wriggled away and fell against the door. Even as she regained her balance, the door opened to reveal Simmy's startled face.

Seeing them together and observing Faye's dishevelled hair, she was secretly delighted. Obviously the courtship was proceeding to her own satisfaction. Simson regarded the Hon Edward's appearance on the voyage as nothing short of divine intervention and deliverance, since it left her free to endure her own considerable discomforts without incommoding her young mistress or upsetting her social activities.

There was another reason. The Earl's son was a particular favourite of hers and she privately thought that Faye should have accepted his proposal. As well as paying her lavish compliments, he was always ready with a sovereign to slip into her hand. Sympathetic to her seasickness, he assured her that she must let it take its course and not worry about a thing. Keep her head down, be as comfortable as possible and he would take good care of Faye.

'Yes I will, Simmy—promise. I'll be chaperon. I can't of course offer to play lady's maid, but that apart—'

Simson decided that things were working out very well, far beyond her expectations. She had even 'put in a good word' for him, as he called it, with Sir Joshua. On that particular occasion she had felt sorry for him for he had confessed that he was wildly in love with Miss Faye.

Simson shook her head. She considered her young mistress was ill-advised not to encourage the young gentleman who was not only an Earl's son, but also handsome—and thoughtful. Her interceding on his behalf had produced a mammoth box of chocolates tied up with red ribbon. She accepted this gift with reproachful gratitude, uncomfortably aware that some might consider it nothing less than a bribe. As if the young gentleman understood her sensibilities, he said immediately:

'Nothing to do with that, Simmy, just because I appreciate your kindness in lending a ready ear to all my troubles. You remind me of Nanny—she was Scotch, like you. Best in the world.'

The Hon Edward *was* a man of honour, thought Simmy. He had given his word that no harm would come to Miss Faye, and as the weather was quite dreadful and she was continually ill, she was glad to seek relief and oblivion by burying her head in her soft pillow fortified by her special sleeping draught.

Simson decided that even her miserable malaise might prove a blessing in disguise and for the sake of romance—which she imagined blossoming a little more with each passing day—she would not rush to plead that she was fit and well again. If her suffering was what the Good Lord intended then she would sit back and await the outcome, especially as Sir Joshua himself would be both delighted and relieved should the shipboard courtship develop into marriage.

The night had been especially fierce and Simmy had fallen at last into an exhausted sleep when early next morning Faye dressed quietly and slipped out of the cabin. She found Captain MacManus's edict about 'staying below decks' utterly unbearable. Besides, she felt as if she would suffocate if she could not breathe fresh air soon. She was the child of generations of mariners and she longed for the feel of ocean winds in her face, the smell of sea-spray.

Cautiously she made her way to the promenade deck. The ship was rolling alarmingly, the sea thudding into her sides, booming, echoing. Faye was glad of the set of the stairs, planned for safety in such weather.

To her chagrin she found the main doors were battened down and locked. It was infuriating to be a prisoner on her own ship like this. She was about to go in search of someone in authority when one of the deck hands appeared through a side door. She leaped forward and he was so astonished that he automatically saluted and held the door open for her. Then he realised her intention, and shouted:

'Miss, come back, come back!' When she did not heed him, the boy decided to make himself scarce. Captain MacManus would have his hide for that.

As soon as Faye left the shelter of the overhang, the wind buffeted into her, almost throwing her off-balance. Fierce gusts hurled themselves against her and she realised why the Captain did not want passengers on deck. Conditions were not only unpleasant but extremely perilous. However, having come this far, she was determined to enjoy—if that was the right word—a few breaths of fresh air before returning to her stateroom. Once she almost slipped on the wet deck. It was frightening and beautiful at the same time. Only herself, a frail girl, witnessing the *Atlanta's* battle with the enraged boiling ocean.

She was not as alone as she imagined . . .

Captain MacManus was exhausted. For the past eighteen hours he had been wrestling with the classic Atlantic winter storm. His seamanship had been tested to the utmost, as from the chartroom he directed the great liner into the currents which would ensure least damage to the ship—and the least inconvenience and discomfort to her passengers.

Every four hours, throughout day and night, as the ship's bell sounded, the wheel changed hands and a new officer came on duty. Captain MacManus however, doggedly refused to leave the bridge.

When First Officer Mason heard of this, he was alarmed. An older, more experienced sailor, he knew the terrible strain the Captain was under. He was shocked by the deathly pale face, the dark glittering eyes sunk into their sockets.

'Are you all right, Captain?' he ventured.

The Captain shrugged. 'Nothing that a good night's sleep won't cure.'

'Then I suggest—'

'No.'

'If you please, Captain, I can take over for a few hours.' First Officer Mason sounded offended.

'I appreciate your motives, Mr Mason, but I shall survive, I promise you that.'

Mason observed that he was staggering, hardly able to keep his feet against the swaying ship. 'No man can keep going in these conditions, all those hours without sleep,' he said gently.

The Captain's slow smile greeted his remark. 'Is that a fact now, Mr Mason? Ah, you've reminded me—it is time for another dose of my medicine.' And the officer saw that he was instantly alert, and had taken from his jacket pocket a small flask.

'*I* can survive—as long as I fortify myself with this.' He grinned, white-faced, at Mason. 'An old sailor's trick which Sir Joshua taught me. You take a small reviving sip every hour—no more, no less. That warms the cockles of your heart—no need to look disapproving, Mr Mason—or are you teetotal?'

Mason shook his head and the Captain continued: 'This is purely for medicinal purposes—no swigs of rum, that would be fatal in my condition—just—one—*small* sip! There.' He corked the flask and straightened his shoulders. 'And now I'm ready for anything, Mr Mason.'

The officer's face was a study. Did the Captain think he could do battle with the Atlantic, run the ship single-handed, if necessary, all the way to Halifax on sips of rum? The older man shook his head sadly as they parted company. He had seen plenty of young Captains like MacManus in his time—proud, ambitious, sure of themselves at the beginning—until they learned that no living man could foil the whims of the sea.

Captain MacManus was not quite ready for the vision that met his eyes on the promenade deck and his composure was shattered by the sight, through a veil of spray, of a woman walking the deck!

Rubbing the window clear, his sense had already informed him that the girl was Faye Wainwright. What

in heaven's name was she about, wandering along the
deck against his orders?

A sudden blast of sea spray again hid her from his
sight. He looked again. She had vanished. He shrugged.
Was he having hallucinations? Besides, how could she
have got on deck with the doors battened? Was the
Wainwright girl getting so much under his skin that he
imagined her presence?

He rubbed his nose thoughtfully. He would be wise to
go easy on that rum—

At that moment he stared down and Faye Wainwright
was still there! As if conscious of his gaze, she turned,
looked up at the bridge and waved. Thunderstruck by
her impertinence, the Captain raised his hand, and
pointed towards the interior of the ship, denoting that
she return thence immediately.

In return, she smiled, indicating the weather with a
despairing face and gesture. Then she walked on.

How dare she defy him? Astonished, he realised she
was totally ignoring his command.

To Faye, of course, he was merely a blurred shape.
Only intuition warned her that it was Captain Mac-
Manus, taking a polite interest in her progress. She was
delighted to be free. Starved of fresh air, she didn't care
how cold and icy the spray, or how fierce the gale. As
long as she could keep her feet, any discomfort was
worth escaping from the claustrophobia of 'below decks'
for a while. After all, she was no hothouse plant. Reared
to a spartan life at Wainwrights, she rode each morning
regardless of weather.

She glanced back at the uniformed figure on the
bridge, alone but for the outline of the duty-officer at the
wheel. In more kindly moments she told herself that the
Captain's dour manner signified a rather shy man, intimidated by the presence of the owner's granddaughter
on this, his first command.

She respected his pride, guessing that he would de-
spise 'kow-towing' to important people, for he was not
the kind who would consider any his betters. For all his
humble background, he had natural good manners, and
sometimes she blushed to remember how badly Teddy

could—and did—behave, how rude he was to servants who did not appear promptly to answer his summons. He was rude to everyone, in fact, except those like Simmy, who might be useful to him. To others, high or low, he did not care in the least what he said, when the mood—or the wine—took him.

On the bridge, Captain MacManus had decided that the Wainwright girl had heeded his command and returned below decks.

The next instant, to his utter amazement, he beheld the top of a hat, firmly secured by a scarf, followed by Faye's smiling face as she struggled up the steps to the bridge. As she came alongside, he was at a complete loss for words.

'I see you are alone—like me.' Her manner was shy, angelic and sweet, as she pointed to the man at the wheel. 'Well—almost. He can't be much company for you in this weather. I expect it takes him all his time—'

'Excuse me,' interrupted the Captain, retaining his temper with difficulty. Swiftly, he marched into the chartroom and closed the door. At least she would take the hint, he would be safe from her there.

'Phew, what a gale. Is it often like this? I never expected to encounter such weather.'

Captain MacManus blinked, stunned. Without so much as a by-your-leave, she had followed him into this holy-of-holies. Pausing for breath, she hesitated, smiling, obviously awaiting an invitation which was not forthcoming.

'Well, may I sit down?' And without waiting for his assent, she flopped down into his chair, studying the sea maps. 'Now, tell me where *exactly* we are.'

Gavin MacManus was speechless. Faye observed his odd appearance, his pale face.

'I say, Captain, you're all right, aren't you?' Staring into the storm, she swallowed hard. It was very nasty indeed out there and this height provided an alarming sensation—quite different from below decks where the only sight of the sea was through portholes.

'Is something awful going to happen?' she whispered. 'You can tell me what it is you fear.'

In answer the Captain turned his back sharply upon her. How dare she! *She* was accusing him, quite plainly, of cowardice. *A coward!* He felt as if he would never speak again as he fought for words that would not come. Only a choice line in Gaelic invective would do—

'I beg your pardon—what did you say?' And without waiting for his reply, she said anxiously: 'There *is* something wrong, I can feel it,' she added solemnly.

'Wrong!' He spat out the word, squared his shoulders and said in icy tones, 'May I remind you, ma'am, that passengers are not allowed on this bridge. It is strictly forbidden—'

'Passengers, Captain?' Her eyes opened wide. 'That surely does not apply to me.'

'It does indeed. The rule was made not by me but by your grandfather. The Wainwright Line orders—'

'Oh, *rubbish*, Captain,' she laughed. 'You know who I am.'

'I do indeed, Miss Wainwright. And I must ask you to leave immediately.'

Faye regarded him coldly. 'May I remind *you*, Captain MacManus, that I am Sir Joshua's granddaughter.'

'I need no reminding, madam—and *damn* your impudence.'

'Don't you dare swear at me!' And Faye leaned back hastily as he towered above her.

'I don't care if you are the Queen of England,' he hissed, '*no* woman, not even the Queen herself, is permitted on *my* bridge.'

'I have business to discuss with you, Captain—business that will not wait.' Faye's tone was commanding. It had no effect.

'If you have business to discuss, then I suggest that you present yourself at my cabin,' he stopped to consult the clock, 'in precisely one hour's time.'

'I shall do nothing of the sort, Captain. The very idea! You will present yourself at *my* stateroom—' Faye had forgotten entirely that she had invented 'business' as an excuse. 'Or—' she added angrily.

The Captain noted the ringing tones of authority which would have caused a lesser man to cower.

'Or,' he supplied, 'you will tell your grandfather all about my beastly behaviour to you. That I have insulted you, shouted at you too. Is that it?'

It wasn't. No threat had been intended. Even if it had she would have changed her mind once her temper cooled. She could never behave in such a mean and selfish way as to take advantage of his position as her grandfather's employee.

Gavin MacManus knew he had won. 'Get off my bridge,' he said roughly and turned his back on her. 'Now, this moment, if you please.'

That was the final straw. How dare he behave like this! Such arrogance! Well, she would show him. She stood up and screamed: 'Don't you dare turn your back on me. I haven't finished with you yet, Captain MacManus.' She seized his arm, at her touch, he spun round to face her. 'I have had just about enough of your rudeness. You may be sure that I will not forget your outrageous conduct—'

At that moment the weather took over their argument. The *Atlanta* seemed to come to a sudden full stop. Then she gave a sickening roll, pitting man-made strength agains the fury of the ocean.

Faye's feet shot from under her. She was propelled into thin air, screaming, and the Captain grabbed her as she fell. They were hurled against the wall, their faces touching.

Now the *Atlanta* righted herself again and Faye found her balance. With the Captain's face only inches from her own, she had made an interesting discovery. The eyes she had thought of as black and angry, were, in fact, dark green, like the weeds swaying at the bottom of a pond.

'Release me—instantly!'

The Captain shook his head and if anything tightened his hold. 'In a moment, Miss Wainwright, in a moment. I haven't finished with *you*, yet.'

'Let me go!'

He smiled slowly. 'Not until you have heard what I've got to say. You, Miss Faye Wainwright, are a spoilt brat. Has anyone ever told you that before?' Without waiting for her reply, he continued, 'In your carefully sheltered existence, you neither know nor care what real life is all about. You think it's having the right dress to wear, the right fork to eat with. And you'll go on believing it, cushioned against the real world, living in a fairytale fantasy, for the rest of your life.'

'How dare you—how *dare* you say such things to me?'

'I dare, Miss Wainwright, because I have nothing to lose. No man owns me—not even your grandfather who I respect as much as any man living. And no woman, either—'

'*That* does not surprise me, seeing your uncouth behaviour. No decent woman would want anything to do with your sort.'

'Is that so?' Still he smiled, and although his voice was soft, gentle almost, she was conscious of his body hard against her own. 'I've seen plenty of your sort of woman, who are not averse to taunting an ordinary man with their charms. Any day on this ship you can see them flaunting themselves—'

'How *dare* you suggest—'

'I dare, Miss Wainwright, I dare. And you are no better than the rest. And since you are going to complain to your grandfather about being insulted, let me give you real grounds for complaint—'

And so saying, he raised one hand and seizing her chin forced it back. Then his mouth descended on hers. Faye could not believe any of this was happening, that he was actually kissing her nor that a kiss could last so long and yet she could go on breathing. At last he released her and held her at arms' length.

'It isn't my best performance, Miss Wainwright. I can do better—I assure you—'

Panting, breathless, she looked up at him and he saw that her eyes were filled with tears. The sight was so unexpected, for he was waiting for rage, fury, assault. Now he was taken aback, humbled, when he should have been most arrogant.

'Are you quite finished?' Her voice was a whisper.

'Quite.'

How indifferent—bored even—he sounded. 'May I leave now?' her own voice was not quite steady.

He bowed. 'Please do.' She had reached the top rung of the ladder which connected bridge with deck when he said: 'One moment, Miss Wainwright.'

Her eyes were reproachful flowers after rain, as she stared back mutely at him.

'I think you should, er—do something—about your hat.'

During their embrace it had come sadly adrift from its mooring scarf and now hung over one ear, a sight which would have struck both of them as comical in any other circumstances. Neither was disposed to mirth at that moment. Faye straightened her hat with a shaking hand, while the Captain watched her solemnly tuck in a final strand of hair.

'Is that correct, Captain? Will that do?'

Unable to find words, he nodded.

'Very well.' Recovering her composure, she stared at him proudly, chin raised. In that steely gaze there was a strong resemblance to Sir Joshua. 'I am leaving now, as you requested. But I think I ought to inform you that the ship *never* behaved in this fashion when my grandfather was in command.'

With those words she moved swiftly down the steps, leaving Captain MacManus torn between the desire to laugh out loud at her outrageous statement and the sudden longing to call her back. To hold her tightly in his arms and kiss her, again and again.

Alone on his bridge, it was too late for apologies, too late to tell her that weary and exhausted by the terrible hours he had spent wrestling with the storm, he needed a woman's comforting arms and a woman's love.

What have I done? he groaned. And conscience told him that whatever else, when Sir Joshua heard of his brutish assault upon his beloved granddaughter, he would relieve him of his command of the *Atlanta*.

He had thrown away his future—he must have been mad—mad with longing and loneliness.

CHAPTER
SIX

WHEN Faye left the Captain's bridge, her feelings were as disturbed as the weather. The encounter had left her emotions in a new and delicious torment. No man had ever kissed her or held her with such passionate intensity before. She was reluctant to go below and leave this fantasy into which those moments on the bridge had plunged her. Soon she would be believing that she had dreamed it all . . .

Suddenly the side door, through which she had come on deck, again shot open. Teddy staggered unsteadily towards her.

'What on earth are you doing here, old girl? I've been searching for you everywhere. Don't you know it's dangerous walking the deck in this weather? Come inside, for heaven's sake.' His exasperated tones, his bossy manner, returned Faye, sharply and unpleasantly, to reality.

'Is everything all right?' he demanded, staring into her face.

'Of course. Why shouldn't it be?' Her voice was colder than Teddy's anxious manner deserved. He gave her a wounded look, as she added: 'I'd like to stay out for a while—I was enjoying the fresh air.'

'Oh, all right. If that's what you want.'

She took his arm against the rolling motion, as they battled upwards along the deck.

'What have you been up to all this time?' His suspicious manner asserted ownership. Faye felt cross. Soon he would be behaving like a jealous husband, before they were even betrothed.

'I felt like taking a stroll—and I decided to have a word with Captain MacManus.'

'But he's on his bridge, Faye.'

'And where else should he be, dear Teddy?' she said, heavily sarcastic. 'Do you know what he *did*?'

Teddy shook his head.

'The wretched man demanded—yes, demanded—that I leave immediately.'

Faye expected Teddy to clench his fists in rage at this insult. He merely nodded. 'Quite right too, quite right, old girl.' He smiled. 'It ain't allowed, y'know. Everybody knows that no one—especially no woman—is ever allowed to set foot on the Captain's bridge.'

'That's ridiculous.'

'Women are reckoned to be bad luck, old girl, thought you would know that. And, besides, it's a company rule.'

Faye sighed. 'Teddy,' she explained patiently, 'I am not everybody. I can't help being a woman—but I am also a Wainwright; this company will belong to me someday—the *Atlanta* will be mine.'

Obstinately Teddy shook his head. 'Makes no difference, m'dear. Even that won't give you the right to go on the Captain's bridge—unless specially invited, of course.' He chuckled. 'And I can't see any Captain doing that—they're a superstitious lot where women are concerned.'

'Grandfather used to take me on the bridge himself, and let me steer the ship. I used to hold the wheel, anyway,' she said, not wanting to sound too pompous.

Teddy grinned. 'You were a little girl then, that was different. I suppose children don't count. Anyway, he was Captain then, it was his business. If he wasn't superstitious, he could also afford to make—or break—the ship's rules.' He paused. 'Was that all that happened?'

'Yes. Why?'

'Oh, you seem very upset about it.'

Faye glanced in the direction of the bridge. 'Not upset—just annoyed.'

'Had enough exercise?' Teddy shivered.

'I suppose so.'

'Then stop looking so glum, m'dear—come along and

have some refreshment. That'll cheer you up no end. Incidentally, the Count has invited us to a hand of cards. An agreeable way of passing the time until luncheon. Don't know about you, but I'm starved.'

Faye accompanied him reluctantly. She hated cards and she could never guess what hands the other players were holding, she forgot what were trumps and she could never remember what was the score or who was winning. Today she played worse than usual, dealing slowly and fumbling the cards, which even succeeded in drawing an exasperated sigh from Teddy who was her partner, and in whose eyes she was normally incapable of error.

Suppressing a yawn, she looked at the other passengers, similarly engrossed. What a picture they made, the ladies in their gowns by Worth and the other great couturiers from Paris; the men tailored by Savile Row. Although jewels were mainly kept for evening, there were plenty of pearls and diamonds in evidence and the result was a dazzling spectacle of colour, the atmosphere perfume-laden, rich and warm with exotic scents mingling with expensive cigars.

A sharp intake of breath, a suppressed curse from Teddy, indicated that she had once again played the wrong card. She apologised. But her mind was miles away.

Teddy scowled across the table. The Count was gleefully victorious. The game was at an end and Teddy declined another hand. He did not like being beaten.

Faye rose from the table. No, she did not wish Teddy to accompany her. Why didn't he join the other gentlemen in the smoking-room?

Huffily Teddy departed and Faye made her way back to her stateroom. Once inside, she sank on to the sofa and decided she must be the only unhappy person aboard. Everyone she met seemed cheerful and entirely confident.

At least poor Simson was not falsely cheerful. She, for one, would be thankful indeed to set foot on dry land again. The voyage, for her, seemed endless.

'You're alone, Miss Faye?' She was surprised not to

see Mr Teddy's face beaming over her young mistress's shoulder.

'Yes,' said Faye shortly and Simson regarded her anxiously. She hoped the two hadn't quarrelled. A few minutes later she was reassured as a knock at the door revealed the caller as Mr Teddy, half-hidden behind a mass of red roses.

There was nothing Faye could do but invite him in. She regretted the roses, her cabin was like a bower already. He whispered they were a 'peace-offering' and she knew that he had bought them from the greenhouses the ship carried and that they had cost a great deal of money.

He turned his attentions to Simmy and plied the maid with anxious questions about her health. Seeing how pleased she was, even to blushing, aglow with pleasure, as he secured one of the roses in the neckline of her blouse, Faye looked at him anew. As if seeing him for the first time, she realised that Teddy Haversham, for all his faults, was really a very pleasant and charming young man. He wasn't a brutish oaf—when sober—and she bristled with sudden anger at the image of Captain MacManus which floated to the forefront of her mind.

'No, I shan't be having lunch today,' she said in reply to Teddy's question. He and Simson regarded her anxiously. Was she feeling quite well? Sure she wasn't under the weather?

Oh why did they make such a fuss, thought Faye in despair as she replied: 'I'm eating too much these days, I simply want to skip an occasional meal. I assure you I am not in the least indisposed. I will see you at dinner, Teddy.'

He could not ignore this dismissal and when he departed, Simson drew the curtains and helped her undress. Gratefully, Faye sank into bed. She did not remember when she had been so tired or dispirited. She wanted only to close her eyes and switch off the whole world.

Simson let her sleep undisturbed even by the arrival of afternoon tea. When she did awake, it was time to bathe

and dress for dinner. She knew at once from Simmy's
face and the gentle motion of the ship that the *Atlanta*
had moved into calmer weather at last.

Refreshed by her slumbers, she decided on the Chantilly lace dress with its pale peach underskirt and matching sash. The high collar was most becoming to her long
slender neck and although the colours were not harmo-
nious, she accepted Simmy's suggestion that she add a
corsage of Mr Teddy's red roses.

Golden hair upswept and held by diamond clasps and
the brooch which was a family heirloom, Simmy stood
back to admire the result of her labours. She concluded
that the brightness of Miss Faye's eyes outshone all the
other jewels and she was fastening the peach satin
evening shoes when there was a tap on the door.

'That will be Mr Teddy, please let him in.'

Faye decided that he was early for once. Inevitably
these days he was late for dinner. Full of apologies,
they were always last to take their seats at the table. The
reason was that Teddy consumed too many drinks in the
smoking-room during the idle hours of the afternoon.
Sometimes he found it difficult to get through the two-
hour-long eating marathon that was their evening meal
at the Captain's table, without dozing off.

But the new arrival was not Teddy.

Faye swung round from the mirror.

'*You!*' she whispered.

Captain MacManus stood in the doorway, cap under
arm. He too was refreshed by a few hours' sleep and he
had come to escort her to dinner, and to apologise for his
outrageous behaviour that morning.

At that moment, looking at the lovely girl before him,
a vision of beauty, of gentle softness and femininity, with
her perfume enveloping his senses, he realised that there
was nothing in the world he would rather have than a
good many more of those delicious kisses. What was he
to say? Some excuse was in order, some smooth speech
which was quite beyond him but would leave his mascu-
line pride and her female vanity both appeased.

Faye was shaken by his unexpected appearance at her
door. 'A moment, if you please, Captain,' she said

stiffly. 'I have the list somewhere. Have you seen it, Simmy?'

Simson and the Captain exchanged bewildered glances. Then Simson remembered a list of complaints her mistress had been composing.

'Here it is, Miss Faye.'

'There you are,' said Faye, thrusting the paper into his hand. He stared at it. 'It was kind of you to remember that I wished to talk to you on business matters. These—' she indicated the paper he held, 'are some of the inadequacies in furniture and equipment of the stateroom and elsewhere on the ship.'

Captain MacManus stared again at the list. 'Toast to be served in a napkin—hot; Notices on board to be restricted to as few as possible and those tastefully framed, not flapping about every time a door opens; Sailing lists and general regulations should be included in passengers' lists; in the stateroom—dirty linen closet is too small—closets in general are inadequate.'

He looked up slowly. 'Is that *all*?'

She was adjusting her diamond earrings in the mirror. 'There is one other thing, Captain, quite a small one but very important to passengers' comfort. The pillows should be softer—plumper.'

'I see,' he said, his face stony.

'Of course, I have learned to live with, and to accept, things like tiny closets. However, I feel that future passengers might not be so tolerant.'

The Captain's instinct was to tear the paper into little pieces, throw it on the floor and stamp upon it. He restrained his feelings admirably, folded the paper neatly and placed it in his pocket.

'I regret you have been dissatisfied, ma'am, and inconvenienced during the voyage. However, I cannot be of help to you in this matter. This is the Chief Steward's department and I will bring it to his attention. I only sail the ship, ma'am,' he added heavily, 'I am not responsible for her furnishings.'

'I realise that, of course, Captain.' Faye looked up at him, her eyes flower-like in the heart-shaped face.

She was superb, he thought. And had she been the

Devil made flesh, he could not stay angry with her. 'I really came—' his voice softened, 'to escort you to dinner, if I may be accorded the Captain's privilege.'

Faye beamed upon him. She would be the centre of all admiring and envious female eyes as she walked down the grand staircase that evening on the handsome Captain's arm.

'How kind,' she said, as her heart thumped in a manner more in keeping with the ocean outside than the calm luxury around her.

He bowed. 'Shall we?' And his slow smile warmed her heart. At the door he extended his arm. She was about to take it when they were disturbed by a noisy upheaval in the corridor. The sound of a crashing tray of crockery and glass was followed by Teddy Haversham's voice raised in angry tones.

'Damn you, blundering fool, look where you're going.'

Murmured apologies followed, but Teddy's altercation with the unseen steward continued. His voice was louder than usual and noticeably slurred. He appeared around the corner, swaying dangerously. When he saw the Captain, he scowled and Faye realised, with some misgivings, that she had never given him a second thought. She was so overwhelmed by the Captain's invitation that she had completely forgotten that Teddy normally escorted her to dinner.

Now there would be another unpleasant scene! Her slight hesitation communicated itself to the Captain, who quickly released her arm: 'I see, ma'am, that I came too late, and that you already have an escort for this evening.'

He bowed over her hand, but this gallant gesture was interrupted as Teddy rudely pushed him aside.

'What's he doing here, Faye? Is he insulting you again.'

At the word 'again' the Captain's eyes narrowed. So she *had* told young Haversham about their encounter on the bridge. He gave her a reproachful glance, disappointed in her, as well as embarrassed and angry. He decided on a hasty withdrawal and bowed politely to them both.

'Wait a minute,' said Teddy. 'You haven't answered my question. I'll call you out, sir, Captain or no, if you keep on pestering this lady with your unwelcome attentions.'

'Teddy—please,' whispered Faye.

As the Captain made to turn away, Teddy grabbed his arm. 'You listen to me—'

Calmly the Captain faced him and, seizing his hand, removed it from his arm, in the distasteful manner of someone who has removed a crawling object. As he did so, he drew himself up to his full height topping Teddy by a couple of inches. 'And you listen to me, sir. Call me out you said? You!' He laughed and his contemptuous glance included Faye, trying hard to look inconspicuous at Teddy's side. 'You two *idiotic children,* do go away and *play* somewhere quiet—and preferably far from my sight. And for pity's sake, do try to keep from under my feet unless you both want to be spanked and put to bed without any supper.'

He turned swiftly on his heel and left them. Teddy's aggressive move to hurtle after him was restrained by Faye.

'Please, Teddy—no scene. Remember who you are, for heaven's sake.'

'You heard what he said—what he called us.'

'I did. And I think for once that we both deserved it.'

Simson who had been a shocked onlooker said in Teddy's defence, 'He shouldn't have called you—that—Miss Faye.'

'It wouldn't have been necessary if Teddy hadn't behaved in such an ungentlemanly way.'

'He didn't, Miss Faye.'

'Simmy, I suggest you keep out of this, Mr Teddy is well able to look after himself, even to the extent of shaming the rest of us by his behaviour.'

'If that's the way you feel,' said Teddy, 'I'm going—this moment.'

Faye had very real fears about how he might behave if he went to the Captain's table in such a belligerent mood. She said: 'Oh, Teddy, don't let's quarrel—over nothing at all. We'll all feel much better after dinner. Come along, there's a good fellow.'

Still grumbling, Teddy promised to let bygones be bygones—for the present. But just let that Captain step out of line *once* more—and he'd give him a thrashing he would not forget.

'I hope before you are ever tempted to do so,' said Faye, 'that you will remember that it is also within his powers to clap you in irons if you abuse him physically in any way. After all he is the law on the *Atlanta*.'

During the elaborate meal that followed Faye avoided looking in the Captain's direction and was glad that her chair did not face him. Occasionally she saw him in profile talking earnestly to his table companions and her heart misgave her. Bitterly she regretted Teddy's appearance just when all was going so well with the Captain, since his arrival to escort her into dinner clearly meant she had been forgiven. She had even detected a tender glance from that stern face. Did that mean he was remembering too? She shrugged away the thought and chided her silly heart for behaving in such a fashion. Not even she could find anything flattering in his behaviour towards her, in fact if she wasn't such an idiot she should be indignant. She thought of the fuss Teddy would make—to say nothing of her Grandfather—if she rushed to them and said the Captain had 'assaulted' her on the bridge. Anyway, she had her pride. No, she reckoned that she deserved it—she had been patronising and rude to him.

As the dinner proceeded and entrée gave place to elaborate desserts, gâteaux that were turreted castles made entirely of ice-cream and icing sugar on the outside, their interiors filled with sponge, more cream and maraschino cherries all heavily soaked in liqueurs, Faye began to imagine that the Captain's brief glances in her direction were faintly hostile.

Perhaps she had dreamed the whole encounter, for she had slept both long and deep for several hours during the day. It was just the sort of dream she might have had of a kiss unlike any other she had ever experienced, a kiss that searched out the depths of her starved emotions as if all the love in her heart had been sleeping, awaiting this magic to set it free, to let her emotions come spilling out, all the true feelings her lady-like exterior, her stern upbringing, had suppressed and denied.

The orchestra was playing a number both familiar and appropriate. 'The Sleeping Beauty' waltz. Faye hid a sigh. Was she like that sleeping princess, waiting all these years for the prince's kiss to rouse her to life and love? She glanced across at the Captain—but he did not fit such an image, he was no prince, he wasn't even an Earl's son like Teddy. Captain Gavin MacManus, whatever the secret feelings he aroused in her, was inaccessible. He was her grandfather's employee. 'Humbly born, but proud as the devil,' the Gaffer had told her. She thought of his background, his life in the Hebrides, a life utterly beyond her imaginings; he might as well have come from another planet.

She shrugged that thought aside, for she need have no worries about any possible future with Gavin MacManus, there was no world which could contain them both in harmony. In a sudden lull in the table talk she saw Teddy and the Captain exchange steely glances and she shivered to think that she might be included in the Captain's anger, that his behaviour indicated that he longed for revenge upon the rich and idle; that his kiss was a calculated insult . . .

She had refused the cheese and was now on the final course—coffee, liqueurs and sweet biscuits. She pushed her plate aside.

'What's wrong?' whispered Teddy. Involuntarily she glanced towards the Captain and Teddy said furiously: 'Don't let him upset you. Wait until the Gaffer hears—he'll give him what's what—cost him his job, like as not. And serve him right,' he added with relish. 'I've never been so insulted—'

'No, Teddy, please. I don't want that. Please, promise now—you won't say anything.'

'Well—' Teddy frowned.

'Please, Teddy—for me.' Her pleading eyes, her hand on his arm, were irresistible.

'Oh, very well. Provided you make it worth my while, of course.' His teasing words belied the glint in his eye. 'Listen—'

The Captain was assuring the table that as long as the calm spell of weather continued, dancing would take place after dinner each evening. Applause greeted his announcement.

Later, dancing with Teddy, Faye saw the Captain take the Countess as his partner. She tried not to glance enviously at them as Teddy sang sentimental songs in her ear, holding her too close for comfort. Once she saw the Countess smile in their direction, murmur something to the Captain who also glanced at them as they waltzed past. He nodded agreement to the Countess and Faye felt her face grow crimson. Doubtless the Captain considered—as did everyone else who witnessed Teddy's possessive manner towards her—that they were lovers.

The thought angered Faye considerably. She observed that the Captain danced superbly, as she might have suspected from his easy graceful movements. Teddy refused to relinquish his hold on her when each dance ended, so Faye had ample opportunity on the tiny dance floor to observe the Captain as he led a succession of ladies through the twists and twirls of the St Bernard's Waltz.

He never put a foot wrong, endowed with a natural rhythm while poor Teddy, graceless as a carthorse, thumped and stumbled and crushed her toes underfoot. He exhibited clear evidence, rather shamingly, Faye observed, as did many other men on the floor, of being at the end of a hard-drinking day.

At one stage, whether by accident or design, Teddy cannoned into the Captain. Faye had to admit it was deliberate for when the Captain bowed politely and apologised, Teddy scowled and muttered about 'calling him out'.

Captain MacManus did not appear much put out by this remark, if he heard it at all, as he carried his partner swiftly along.

One novelty number was a 'Lady's Choice', considered rather fast and daring, although all it did was to give the various unescorted ladies at each table the chance to dance.

To Faye's surprise the Countess asked Teddy and as the couples drifted from the table she found herself sitting alone opposite the Captain. She looked nervously in his direction, but head averted, he stiffly studied the dancers, as if his life depended on it.

How she longed to dance with him after Teddy's blundering performance. Suddenly, as she looked across, the Captain's seat was empty. He was coming round to her side of the table.

He held out his arm, smiled.

In silence they walked on to the floor together and the next moment Faye was in his arms. She felt light as thistledown, for she had never before experienced a dancing partner so light upon his feet. Their every movement seemed to dovetail, as though hands and feet and bodies had been specially schooled for each other— and for this moment.

Impossible to imagine that they had never before danced together and that their bodies were strangers to one another. In and out they weaved in a pattern of perfection, firmly confident, without a single false step. It was as if they clearly read each other's thoughts without a word being said; as if both responded to some mysterious signal to unleash movements and skills of which they were unconscious, dictated by a celestial puppet-master.

What shall I talk to him about? That had been Faye's moment of panic when they took to the floor. Now it didn't seem important. No conversation was required of them when their bodies spoke the language of the dance so expertly. Words would have been an intrusion, the magic of the timeless moments they shared would simply have been spoilt.

Faye was only faintly aware of that other world close by, of other dancers who talked and laughed. Once she glimpsed Teddy glowering over at them, but she closed her eyes firmly, refusing to acknowledge his existence on the same magic planet.

If only this moment could last for ever—

Sadly she realised that the music had stopped. The Captain had released her. He was bowing, politely thanking her. Faye joined in the dancers' applause at the end of the item, furiously hoping that the band would consider this worthy of an encore. But no, a final chord and the Captain was leading her back to her place at the table.

'That was a great pleasure, ma'am. Thank you.'

Oh, why did he have to spoil it all now by being so formal?

Teddy hovered close by, his attitude threatening.

Captain MacManus bowed stiffly once again and left them.

'I bet you were bored to death with *him*,' said Teddy at his retreating figure. 'Poor Faye, I thought that dance would never end—I wondered how in the world I was going to rescue you from his clutches.' As they sat down, he flung one arm possessively about her shoulders. 'Glad to get back to me, are you, darling?'

Faye smiled, smoothing her gloved hand which was still warm from the Captain's touch. She heard his voice, bidding the guests goodnight, as he walked round the table.

'Miss Wainwright.'

'Goodnight, Captain.'

As he bowed and vanished from her line of vision, she remembered that as he left he had, very gently and almost tenderly, squeezed that gloved hand.

The gesture spoke volumes in a language of its own. As well as thanking her, it begged forgiveness and told her that the Captain understood perfectly the little world of unspeaking tenderness which they had discovered together.

CHAPTER
SEVEN

THE *Atlanta* had passed the point of no return. In three days she would be in Halifax and Faye doubted whether any of the passengers would be as glad as herself to see land again.

This winter voyage had been charged with emotion, a far cry from the relaxing holiday she had anticipated, and which the Gaffer had promised. Her old dream of sailing again with him as Captain, obviously belonged to the myths of childhood, where everything is distorted by the passage of time.

Present-day reality was far from that carefree voyage, when as a little girl Faye had been the darling of the crew. On off-duty moments she remembered how they had tried to please her with gifts of good things to eat from the galley, or had shyly given her hand-carved wooden toys, made in their leisure hours.

How important she had been then, made to feel like a princess, loved and cherished by everyone. Even the *Atlanta* herself had changed with the years. She was more luxurious now but somehow more impersonal too.

None of these facts, Faye realised, should have interfered with her enjoyment. There was a deeper reason which disturbed her, a feeling of disquiet at the back of her mind. Worried about the Gaffer, she could not shake off her uneasiness. She longed for news of him, to hear his voice again. And her journey away from him had just begun. The plan was that she would return to Wainwrights in time for Christmas.

Yes, she would be glad to reach Halifax. She looked forward to meeting Dulcie Schroeder who was to act as chaperon at her brother's home in New York and would travel with them to Virginia.

The calmer weather encouraged passengers to participate in deck games. Faye went as observer, but could not escape Teddy for long. He soon found her and urged her to join another couple playing shovelboard.

They were losers but for once this did not upset Teddy as he took Faye's arm and they strolled along the deck. The sea was like a mirror.

'Let's hope it stays like this for the rest of the voyage,' was the universal hope from everyone they encountered.

From his bridge, Captain MacManus watched them. He knew a moment's envy for their closeness, their heads together in deep conversation. He was glad the girl had forgiven him for his outburst. Although Haversham still reacted unpleasantly whenever they met, he was apparently restrained from more violent action by Faye Wainwright. She smiled and talked to him politely, as if nothing untoward had happened.

Strange girl she was. But he would have to watch out for that quick temper of his. Passionate outbursts were not advisable for Captains of passenger liners . . .

'Weather's changing, Captain. There's fog ahead—a great bank of it.'

The Captain groaned as he studied the shrouded horizon through his binoculars. The signs were all only too familiar. In a very short while visibility beyond the ship's rail would be less than a hundred yards.

He cursed this new turn of the weather just as they had got the ship's engines up to pressure and were making good progress. He had watched the charts with satisfaction as the sea miles piled up, and he realised that, despite their bad beginning, a turn of good luck and good weather, combined with the new engine power, might put the bounty within his grasp.

Now, once more, the cards were stacked against him. The fog was closing in rapidly and the passengers on deck had become aware of the change in temperature. Shivering now, they huddled into top coats and furs as the foghorn began to bleat doefully—a warning to any ships invisible in the area.

Reluctantly the passengers deserted the games area and some rapidly retreated into the comfort and warmth below decks. The steerage passengers remained on their deck, well out of sight of the first-class area, and the Captain heard the sound of a fiddle, a mouth organ. He realised that out of their cramped uncomfortable quarters and able to walk and breathe free, unpolluted air, it would take something more than a heavy mist to dampen their spirits.

The fog enveloped them. Captain MacManus from long experience suspected that there was something else out there too, concealed as yet. A moment later he was giving the order to change course.

'Isn't it turning bright all of a sudden?' said Faye.

'The sun's getting through—at last,' said Teddy.

'Look—over there—' a voice called and all heads swivelled round, following the direction of the pointing hand.

A large white mass, sparkling with light, veered towards them through the fog.

'Another ship, is it?'

'Yes. Over there—'

Faye and Teddy joined the little group by the rail. 'We haven't seen a ship for days. How lovely,' said Faye peering into the light surrounding a distant white blur.

'It's heading straight for us,' said Teddy. Then, his face white, he yelled: 'My God, we're going to collide—'

The passengers fled, screaming along the deck, as the Captain's voice thundered through the megaphone:

'All passengers return to their cabins immediately.' And seeing the rout below, he added, 'Keep calm—please keep calm. It isn't a ship—I repeat—it is *not* a ship you're seeing out there. It's a small iceberg, but everything is under control.'

'An iceberg!'

Now that the approaching object was not a ship, there was a renewal of interest and curiosity.

Again the Captain's voice: 'The iceberg is drifting away from us. I repeat there is no danger and no need for panic, but please for the time being—will all passengers return below decks. There may be some disturbance from subterranean currents—'

The passengers hardly heeded his words.

An iceberg! They were intrigued. Field glasses were produced and, far from diminishing, the little crowd on deck was increased by curious passengers emerging from salon and cabin.

'An iceberg, did you say? How thrilling.'

The Captain groaned as their ranks grew, for he had not spoken the entire truth. He did not want to alarm them unnecessarily but surely some of them realised that a rogue iceberg could do a lot more damage than a manageable ship.

He cursed that damned fog again, which had concealed it until almost too late. As he felt the *Atlanta* change course, he prayed fervently that this evasive action was not too late to avert a collision between the massive bulk of the ship and the iceberg, at the point where their paths might cross. For he had no means of assessing how much of the iceberg's girth was hidden by fog, or was projecting from the sea.

For the first time Gavin MacManus put all his trust and the lives of his passengers into the power of Sir Joshua's new engines. He threw down the compasses, gave the order:

'Full steam ahead!'

The mighty engines responded to his command and five minutes later—the longest five minutes in the Captain's whole life, although the passengers would never know it—they had beaten the iceberg by less than an eighth of a mile.

'Well done, Captain, well done,' whispered First Officer Mason, wiping his brow. '*That* was a bit too close for comfort.'

'It was only very small, of course,' said Teddy at luncheon.

Captain MacManus overhearing, realised with amazement that the passengers were rather disappointed, that they felt cheated by their brief glimpse of the iceberg—almost as if he had deprived them of a close look at the Statue of Liberty. He shook his head in bewilderment. Not one of them apparently realised that the ship—and their lives had been in mortal danger.

'Your Captain was in an awful hurry to run away,' sneered Teddy.

Faye, who had heard stories of this nightmare for mariners, shuddered and, out of Teddy's earshot, she asked Captain MacManus: 'How big *was* your small iceberg?'

'About four times the size of the *Atlanta*.'

'I thought as much. Grandfather has told me all about the frightful damage they can do. I realise that we were all in deadly peril, whatever the others thought.' She smiled. 'And that some quick thinking took place! I was scared far more than by any storm.'

The Captain looked at her with renewed respect.

She smiled. 'Don't blame them too much, Captain. It's their one bit of excitement on a dull voyage.'

'It's the kind of excitement I can well do without, Miss Wainwright.'

With the iceberg behind them, he should have felt easy, but the unhappy feeling of disquiet continued. Normally he resisted his Hebridean heritage of premonitions, but this feeling grew stronger by the hour and refused to lessen when normal conditions were resumed. He was certain that there was more danger afoot—he could almost smell disaster in the air.

Gales, fog, an iceberg—what next?

All his senses were on full alert, waiting for the next catastrophe.

It came as they finished dinner. The powerful lights of the liner had picked up a small boat.

The engines were stopped, the small boat brought alongside and its passengers unloaded. Women and children, and some injured seamen, their faces blackened from an engine-room explosion—about thirty souls in all. And only one spoke English.

'We are from the Russian steamship *Odessa*, Captain,' said one of the injured seaman and MacManus recognised the insignia of first engineer on the burnt and blackened uniform.

'What happened?'

Amid the weeping women, the wailing children, he heard a sorry tale.

'We were taking emigrants to Halifax in Nova Scotia. The weather was foul and then we hit the iceberg in the fog—'

'We saw it.'

The engineer shook his head. 'The *Odessa* was holed badly, listing heavily and our captain insisted that the women and children and the injured—' The man's face was ashen with pain and Captain MacManus laid a steadying hand on his shoulder, 'that we—take to the boats.'

'Was yours the only boat?'

'No, Captain—there was another one launched.'

'What about the ship—anyone see it go down?'

'No, sir.'

The man groaned again—his head lolled forward.

'I'll have the doctor take a look at your leg, right away.'

'No, Captain—I can wait, there's a lot worse hurt—and burned too in the engine-room explosion—'

'Take these passengers below decks, Mr Mason,' said Captain MacManus to the First Officer. 'I'm turning over No 3 hold as quarters for them—take the injured to sick bay—I presume there are none of our passengers there just now.'

'No, Captain.'

'One thing more,' he said to the engineer who had raised his head again, 'How long ago did this happen?'

'Just before dark.'

Captain MacManus returned to the chartroom and took a bearing on the possible whereabouts of the Russian ship. 'About there, I think', he said triumphantly. His waiting officers shook their heads.

'Like as not at the bottom of the sea by now—and that other boat too, Captain.'

'They'll never survive in this weather,' said Mason.

'What about the ones we've just picked up?' the Captain demanded. 'Of course the second boatload will survive—if we can reach them in time and they don't have to stay in the open all night.'

'Do we steam ahead, Captain?'

'No, dammit, we don't. We're going back.'

'But Captain—'

'There's just a chance. Reverse engines—'

'Aye, aye, Captain.'

By the time Captain MacManus went down to the sick bay, Dr Moore had the worst casualties in hand, and the stewards were somewhat ham-fistedly applying bandages at his instructions.

The engineer, reinforced by a stiff rum, was awaiting his turn. 'Little better now, Captain, thank you. Leg's not broken, but I'm afraid it still hurts like hell.'

'Bad luck, Mac, that'll put you out of action at sea for a while.'

The man stared at him, shook his head. 'My name isn't Mac, sir, it's Bain.'

The Captain grinned. 'Aren't all Scottish engineers called Mac?'

The engineer smiled. 'I'd almost forgotten—been so long away from my native shore. Nearly twenty years serving on the *Odessa*. It's good to hear my own lingo again.'

Dr Moore was approaching and the Captain said: 'Before I leave you in his care, I thought you might like to know that the *Atlanta* is going back to look for survivors from your ship.'

'God bless you, Captain,' the man whispered.

The news that the *Atlanta* was steaming back was met with mixed feelings from the passengers. Some agreed that it was the only possible decision that the Captain could take, but others more selfishly inclined disagreed strongly. Especially passengers like Teddy Haversham, who had taken large smoking-room bets that the *Atlanta* would break the existing speed record for a Royal mail steamer to Halifax.

'We're making good time,' an officer assured Teddy. 'With these engines we can still pick up survivors and get there ahead of schedule.' he added confidently.

'If there are any survivors,' grumbled Teddy. To Faye he said: 'It shouldn't be allowed. They'll all be dead or drowned by now. A waste of time, criminal it is.'

Faye shuddered at his callous remark. 'But what if

some of them are still alive—and hurt—in an open boat in such seas.'

'Oh, shut up, you know nothing about such things, Faye,' said Teddy rudely and stalked off to find a more sympathetic listener.

On the bridge Captain MacManus was fully aware when he gave the order to reverse engines that he had almost certainly thrown away all hope of the bounty. He had destroyed Sir Joshua's dream and his own reward of one thousand pounds. A gamble, against the lives of the crew of the *Odessa*—if they still lived. If there were no survivors then he might well have thrown away his future with the Wainwright Line, for ship-owners did not look kindly on failures, especially when the vast fortune spent on the new engines was also in jeopardy.

As for Faye Wainwright, she was proud of the Captain's gallant action, ashamed of Teddy's mean-mindedness, that a bet could mean more to him than the rescue of human souls. She had watched the rescue, the poor injured seamen being carried below decks and the weeping, ragged, drenched women and terrified children, shivering against the icy wind. She hurried back to her stateroom and asked the startled Simson to produce all the warm clothes she had brought and would prob-ably never wear on the voyage.

'Just heap them on the bed. Yes, warm petticoats, those nightdresses—and yes, shawls, thick stockings—those jackets and camisoles—'

'What on earth are you doing, Miss Faye?' asked the maid as Faye bundled the clothes together.

'I'm taking these down to those poor Russian women, Simmy. They need them more than I am ever likely to.'

'But, Miss Faye—' The door closed rapidly on Sim-son's protests.

The elevator bore her swiftly downwards. She knew the geography of the ship now and, led by the sound of voices and the bustle within, soon found the sick bay. On and down again she found the refugees huddled together for warmth among sacks and spare blankets.

Shyly she went forward, handing out garments to the women. They seemed unable to believe that they were being offered gifts. There were no words they knew to thank her, but overflowing eyes, worn hands that sought and held hers, were eloquent with gratitude. Soon there was delighted laughter as they held up tweed skirts, warm wool jackets, cashmere shawls.

One woman, no older than Faye herself, held a new baby in her arms while a two-year-old girl with her head bandaged clung, eyes closed, to her mother's skirts. She awoke screaming as Faye's shawl was being tucked around her. Bewildered by her surroundings, she was inconsolable. Her mother sought to comfort her and Faye took the tiny baby from her arms as she did so.

It was thus Captain MacManus found her. He hardly recognised the downbent head, the fair hair hiding her face, as she rocked the baby in her arms, crooning to it gently. As his shadow touched her, she clutched the baby closer in the age-old instinct of woman and stared up at him with frightened eyes. His heart smote him and then a glance of recognition passed between them—of recognition and something more—from these two inhabitants of different worlds who could say so little in words without scorching each other with their anger and misunderstanding; and yet, who could also speak volumes of tenderness in one glance.

For Faye that moment was significant. The man whose shadow bent over her belonged to a fantasy and yet she knew that it was such a man whose wife she should have been, whose child she might have held at her breast. How proud she would have been!

But not a word passed between them, their eyes suddenly evaded each other and the moment was lost.

'What are you doing down here, Miss Wainwright?' The words were an effort, their tone unnecessarily sharp.

Faye pointed to the remaining garments being distributed by the elder women. 'I thought that as I have no closets, nor indeed am I likely to have, then these poor souls might well benefit by my own misfortune.' Her bantering tone challenged him.

A gale of laughter came from one corner as an old woman held up a pair of dainty lace-edged drawers and in the mistaken idea that this was some kind of a blouse, tried in vain to force her head through. Faye blushed as the Captain's lips twitched in amusement. Seeing Faye's expression, he hastily turned away.

'You should not be here, Miss Wainwright.'

Faye regarded him angrily. 'I am only trying to help.'

'I realise that your motives are of kindness, but until the doctor has dealt with the injured men and completed his examination of these people—' he paused and looked at her anxiously. 'We don't want an epidemic sweeping the ship—'

Faye shrugged aside his explanation. 'Are there any seriously injured, Captain?'

'I'm afraid so. The Doctor says that it is touch and go with several of the ones who are badly burnt unless they can get proper treatment.'

'But that's terrible—' 'Terrible, is it?' He sounded irritable. 'We are not equipped as a hospital ship, Miss Wainwright—and Dr Moore cannot manage single-handed as he does on a normal cruise with mostly healthy hearty people, whose sole illness is seasickness or indigestion through over-eating.'

'You have no nurse on board?'

'The Wainwright Line's rules are against carrying female personnel.'

And Faye recalled her grandfather's edict: Female members of crew would not be employed—male stewards only—with some scanty knowledge of first-aid and home nursing, in case of emergencies.

'I think you should return to your stateroom, Miss Wainwright.' He looked around. 'These women seem healthy enough, but you never know, there might be sickness—'

'Oh, don't be ridiculous, Captain. I'm not afraid of sickness. I've had measles, chickenpox, scarlet fever—and survived all of them,' she said handing the baby back to its mother.

But Captain MacManus had her firmly by the arm. 'Nevertheless those are my orders. Now please do as you are told, there's a good girl.'

It was worse than insulting being patronised like this, thought Faye furiously, treated like a spoilt child.

'Don't think your generous impulse is not appreciated—'

'Oh, forget it, Captain. That was nothing. I can buy lots more pretty things when we reach New York. I'll never miss those ones—they are quite unimportant.'

Captain MacManus was alone on his bridge. The *Atlanta's* powerful searchlights had swept the sea for the past two hours in the vicinity of the *Odessa's* last known position. They continued to reveal nothing but drifting yellow fog—not even a floating log in token of the disaster.

'It's hopeless, Captain,' said the duty-officer, 'there's nothing out there.'

The Captain stared at the empty sea and realised that if he gave the order to resume their normal course, he might still have the speed record within his grasp. These engines were first-class, in smooth seas they made excellent time, and with luck—

He could always salve his conscience by saying, well, he had tried, and get someone else to break the news of 'no survivors' to the forlorn bereft women and weeping children who waited below.

He shook his head. No, he couldn't do it, not with this instinct, this mere pinpoint of hope to urge him on.

'Full steam ahead. We'll follow the drift of the current until daybreak and if we see no evidence by then—we'll resume course for Halifax.'

The sun was rising over a heavy sea when the lights picked up a dark blob riding the waves near the horizon.

'That's them!'

'Full steam ahead!'

The Captain's hunch had paid off. But there was only one boat. Acting as interpreter, Bain the engineer limped on deck, and told the Captain that after the second explosion; the *Odessa* had gone down with the Captain and most of her crew.

'Fine men they were, sir,' said Bain sadly. 'God bless them.'

Now the Russian emigrants were on deck too, tearfully reunited with their menfolk in that chilly dawn. They had never expected to meet again on this earth and Captain MacManus was the hero of the hour, his hand grasped by one and all in tearful gratitude. The steerage passengers of the *Atlanta* who had witnessed the rescue added their voices:

'Three cheers for our Captain!'

'Hip, hip, hooray.'

Faye had been unable to sleep and, hearing the commotion of rescue, had come on deck. Prudently she decided to remain in the shadows but the scene, the emigrants' emotion, moved her deeply.

At last the Russian families drifted below. The Captain was once more alone, leaning on the rail, staring at the sky, a solitary figure who saw reflected in the dawn the shattering of his own personal dream.

No use brooding. He shrugged away the bitterness of disappointment. After all, he was young and strong. He would get another ship someday, perhaps never again a luxury liner like the *Atlanta*. Not a ship where fifty poor Russian emigrants were weighed against their equivalent in stocks and shares, or a bet to be won or lost. He could do without a ship like that—

'Captain!'

He turned round, whispered: 'Faye!'

She was like a wraith running across the deck towards him.

'I couldn't sleep—I saw it all.'

'Did you, Faye?'

His use of her first name was quite involuntary and she shivered with pleasure.

'Yes, I saw what you did.' Impulsively she stretched out her hands to him. He took them, clasped them warmly in his own. 'I just want you to know that Sir Joshua would have been proud of you. As I am—very proud.' And standing on tiptoe, her lips brushed his cold cheek in gentle salute.

Captain MacManus smiled down at her. 'Sir Joshua will be less than pleased when he realises that my action sacrificed the *Atlanta's* speed record to Halifax.'

'But—the new engines?'

'Even engines cannot fight time.' He stared across the sea. 'How would you choose then, Miss Wainwright? Fifty human souls against a piece of paper? How would you enjoy that on your conscience?' And without waiting for her reply, he swiftly climbed the steps to the bridge.

CHAPTER
EIGHT

When Faye returned to her stateroom, she found Simson all concern for the Russian survivors.

'Oh, miss, those poor men in the water all that time! Awful burns—and broken bones too, some of them. Who's going to care for them, nurse them? And those poor scared women and bairns—'

'There's a doctor on the ship, Simmy,' Faye reminded her.

'One doctor, with a full sick bay.' Simson shook her head. 'He'll never manage. Steward said he'll need help or they'll be dead before we reach Halifax.' She gave Faye a sidelong glance. 'The Captain has put out an appeal for anyone with experience of nursing.'

'Oh good,' said Faye, 'that should help.'

'Miss Faye, he said that only a couple of women from steerage came forward. And they haven't the right kind of knowledge—or the nursing skill that's needed.'

'That's too bad, Simmy, but what can we do?' She looked at the maid's downcast face, as she sat very still, her arms stiffly at her side. Despite her tense attitude, her face was flushed, excited even.

She picked up the hairbrush and twisted it nervously in her hands. 'Miss Faye—' she began, then she shook her head.

'Yes, Simmy. Go ahead. What is it?'

Slowly, the maid began to brush Faye's hair. 'It's nothing, miss, just a notion I had. I don't expect it would ever work, though. Not now.'

'Of course!' said Faye. 'I'd forgotten—*you* used to be a nurse, before you came to Wainwrights.'

'Aye, Miss, and a very good one, though I say it myself, but it's a long time ago—'

'Do you think you could help, Simmy?' asked Faye eagerly.

'Well, yes and no. I mean, I can't neglect my duty to you, Miss Faye. Sir Joshua would never forgive me, after all I promised him—'

'Oh, forget Sir Joshua, for heaven's sake. You want to go, don't you—'

'Yes, miss, but not,' she added soberly, 'if that means inconveniencing you.'

'What absolute rubbish, Simmy. Of course you must go. Here you sit in the cabin all day, waiting to attend to me, while I'm off enjoying myself, gallivanting with Mr Teddy. You must go, you know. You have a greater duty than attending to one girl when men's lives are in danger, when injured sick people need you.' She paused. 'You really didn't think I could be that selfish, surely,' she added gently.

Simmy leaned over and hugged her. 'Not you, miss— never.'

'Off you go, then. Yes, *now*! Put down that brush! I can manage perfectly. Perhaps I can come and help, if you'll show me what to do—I'd like to.'

'Out of the question, Miss Faye. You need proper experience, besides I wouldn't dream of letting a lady like you take care of strange men—' Simson paused, embarrassed, 'it's different for us nurses, miss, but your grandfather wouldn't be at all pleased if I let you help—'

At the door she paused. 'Now you are certain sure, miss, you don't mind me going?'

'Off with you!' Faye smiled.

'God bless you, Miss Faye.'

The news that Simson had gone to help the doctor pleased Teddy very much when he found Faye alone in her cabin. Faye imagined that this was genuine regard for the injured men, but in truth, Teddy did not care in the least for their welfare, only the fact that having Simson out of the way made Faye much more vulnerable to his attentions. That empty stateroom, so inviting, was like a magnet.

'Let's stay here—we can have luncheon delivered.

Aren't you tired of always dining with a tableful of boring other people?'

Faye's eyebrows raised in mockery. 'You always seem to enjoy their company, Teddy. This is news to me.'

'Well, I'm not feeling very sociable today, except,' he stroked her bare arm, 'for your delightful company.'

Faye evaded his hold and hurried to the door. 'I don't wish to stay here, Teddy. What would people say?'

'Say—what should they say?'

'Well, we aren't either engaged or married,' she reminded him gently, 'so it's hardly proper to have our meals in private.'

'We could be engaged, Faye, this minute—I've asked you often enough—why not say yes?'

Faye shook her head. 'I'm not ready to say yes, Teddy.'

Simmy arrived back in time to dress her mistress for dinner. She seemed strangely quiet, thought Faye, and yet filled with suppressed excitement. A totally different Simmy, as if she had stepped at last into a new world and found that it belonged to her.

'Well, tell me all about it?'

But Simson's answers to her questions were vague, as if she was speaking from a far-off country and although she prepared Faye's toilette with her usual skill, her mind seemed elsewhere.

'That's splendid, Simmy,' said Faye. 'Now off you go, back to your patients—that is, if you're not too tired.'

'Oh no, miss, not in the least.' Simson brightened immediately. 'Perhaps I ought to stay with them overnight—there's a lass giving birth any time now. If that's all right by you, Miss Faye,' she added anxiously.

'Of course it is. You do exactly what you wish, Simmy.'

In the dining-room, Captain MacManus's gallantry and his skill in finding and rescuing the remaining survivors from the *Odessa* was the sole topic on everyone's lips. His action was sincerely applauded by all but the sullen few who, like Teddy, had torn up pieces of paper and cursed losing bets all for a few Russian sailors.

Until dinner that night, Faye had not seen the Captain since the survivors came aboard. She was feeling some embarrassment at her daring—carried away so completely by his bravery and the moment—that she had actually kissed his cheek!

She watched in admiration as many of the passengers came by to congratulate the Captain. Some with experience of the sea, commended his skill in evading that iceberg in the first place. They knew all about wild oceans and rogue icebergs!

Faye enjoyed witnessing this new version of Captain MacManus, a man to be respected and admired, although she did not understand him in the least. And, it seemed, she never would since he kept her severely at arms' length. Only in the occasional unguarded glances that passed between them—as when they had danced together—did she feel a deeper unspoken recognition.

As the floor was cleared for dancing, she watched the Captain, hopeful that he would claim her as partner and envious of those who he took to the floor. She watched them return to the table, talking and smiling, but he never came to her. With others he was completely at ease, she discovered, as she danced past with Teddy holding her too close, bruising her toes through their thin satin covering. Captain MacManus did not even glance in her direction, let alone ask her to dance.

She made up her mind and eagerly awaited the Lady's Choice. When it came, she was too shy to rush to his side and, heart hammering, she prayed that none of the other ladies would ask him first. Teddy was claimed by the Countess, others drifted from the table and suddenly she was alone—but for the Captain, solemnly studying the dancers on the floor.

Faye took a deep breath, left her seat and slowly approached him. 'Captain—may I?' She held out her hands, hardly daring to believe that in a few moments they would be dancing together, repeating the magic they had experienced on the last occasion, before their meeting with the survivors of the Russian ship.

The Captain was looking at her, as if unable to believe

his eyes. Hastily he stood up, buttoned his jacket and bowed.

'You must forgive me, Miss Wainwright. It's duty before pleasure tonight, I'm afraid. Will you excuse me, please.' And turning on his heel, he walked quickly away, weaving a path around the dancing couples.

Faye sat down where she was, hardly able to restrain her tears of disappointment and rejection. The Purser who had been sitting at the next table came across and asked her to dance.

'Yes, of course, I'd be delighted,' she said, hating her false smile.

'Not like you to be deserted, Miss Wainwright,' he said teasingly. 'I've been waiting for a chance like this all evening.'

As she listened to the Purser's chatter, she felt as if her heart would break, her misery out of all proportion to the event. Doubtless the Captain had spoken the truth, but she felt slighted, as if he had seized 'duty' as an excuse not to dance with her. But why? Did he hate her so much? She couldn't understand his reaction, certain that he had enjoyed dancing with her—and that strange wordless communication of two people whose bodies are in perfect harmony, one with another.

At last the dance was over and Teddy returned to her side grumbling about the Captain. 'No one can talk of anything else but your precious Captain. No one cares that his so-called gallant action has cost me a mint of money—and mine was by no means the largest bet.'

'How much did you lose?'

'Five hundred guineas.'

Five hundred guineas, thought Faye, in disgust. A fortune to any of the steerage passengers or the Russian emigrants—more than most could hope to earn in a lifetime.

'No thanks Teddy, I don't want to waltz this time. I'd like to return to my cabin.'

'Delighted, my dear, delighted. Your wish is my command.' As they walked along the deserted corridor, she resisted his amorous attempts and held him skilfully at arms' length. When she made it plain that she was going into her cabin to bed—alone—he said sulkily:

'I thought you liked me, Faye. It appears I am wrong.'

'Of course you're not—I like you very much.'

'You don't seem to want my companionship.'

'I do, Teddy, I do. I want us to stay friends.'

He scowled: 'Friends? What sort of relationship is that between the two of us? Have you no red blood in your veins at all? Sorry—sorry—I didn't mean that—honestly. Oh Faye, darling,' he seized her arms, 'Have you no feelings for me at all?'

'Teddy dear, I keep telling you, but you won't listen. I am very fond of you, it's been marvellous having your companionship on this voyage. I don't know what I would have done without you—you have been so very kind.'

As Teddy brightened she had to add hurriedly: 'But I don't want you as a suitor.'

'That's all right, Faye. I don't want to be your suitor—I want to be your husband. Surely you realise that I adore you. Faye, I'm asking you again, to be my wife.'

Faye looked up at him and her eyes filled with tears. Taking this as a hopeful sign, he tried to gather her into his arms. She pushed him away, rather too forcibly.

'Please, Teddy—don't. Don't.'

'Why not, dammit, why not?'

'Because—because—oh I don't know.'

'Why are you crying then?'

'It isn't—well, every day, a girl receives a proposal, Teddy—'

'Then you do love me, just a little. Say you do—and I'll be content to wait.'

'Teddy dear, I like you, oh so much, more than almost anyone else I know.'

'Well then?'

'That's not enough, not for me, for marriage. I want—I have to have—something much more than liking.'

'Faye, don't you realise that lots of girls think exactly as you do. My sister Amelia, for one, and now she's happy as a lark, yet even the day before her wedding, she cried and cried. But she knew she couldn't wait for all that romantic nonsense you girls read in books. Life just isn't like that, so she took old Felix and now they are just like turtle doves.'

Faye looked at him. By no stretch of the imagination could she see herself as Teddy's wife being anything else but grateful—and miserable.

'You see, Faye, let me explain. It's, er, different for a chap. Well, I mean,' he continued, embarrassed. 'Women have to be awakened, their senses you know, by a lover—and that's what marriage will do. I'm a good lover,' he whispered, 'I could make you very happy.'

Faye suppressed a shudder at the picture this offered. With difficulty she summoned a smile. 'I'm too tired to think about it tonight, Teddy. Please, no more argument,' she put a finger to his lips. 'I'm really very tired. Goodnight, Teddy dear.'

As she was closing the door, he said forlornly:

'Besides, the Gaffer would be delighted. You know his heart is set on you accepting me, m'dear. Don't you think you owe him a little happiness too?'

Faye's wan face stared out at him, pensive and somehow tragic.

'And Simson too,' he said eagerly. 'She's a dear soul and she would be so pleased. She could come and live with us—I'd like to have her around. She could still be your lady's maid—I wouldn't be jealous like some husbands and make you take new servants—'

'Goodnight, Teddy.'

Faye leaned thankfully against the closed door as she heard his footsteps retreat into silence. What absurd reasons Teddy presented as to why she should marry him. As she undressed she felt like laughing for the first time. What had her grandfather, her maid, to do with the man to whom she gave the rest of her life? What did either of them know about husbands to begin with?

They would not have to live with her husband day after day, night after night. As she pulled the nightgown over her head, she decided that the days might be lived through quite agreeably with Teddy, but it was the nights that troubled her most of all. How could the Gaffer or dear Simmy understand in a thousand years that marriage for her had to be more than just finding a partner whom society considered suitable.

If she could not be wildly in love, she thought, stroking her neck and her lightly covered bosom, if she could not have a love she would willingly die for, then she would rather not marry at all. Being an 'old maid' did not hold as many worries as being tied to a detested husband, whom one could neither love, cherish nor willingly obey.

She remembered expressing these sentiments to her grandfather. The old man had been quite shocked by such passion in the normally docile and obedient girl he still regarded as little more than a schoolgirl. He had shaken his head sadly, wondering what on earth young folk were coming to these days.

'In my day, girls did what they were told, obeyed their parents and guardians and took the husband who was chosen for them. And if they weren't wildly happy—and few mortals are, my girl—then they made the best of a bad thing, had plenty of children to keep their minds off their own selfish desires for happiness.' Sir Joshua had been truly shocked; such ideas as Faye expressed did not seem quite decent to him.

To him, the main point of marriage was that dynasties were continued and heirs begotten, and property secured.

Faye held her peace after that. For she had always secretly cherished notions of a masterful man, a Heathcliff, a Mr Rochester. And suddenly she clenched her fists.

She realised that at last she had met one man who answered every one of her list of requirements. More, he even attracted her physically in the strongest possible manner. She was more than a little afraid of the power he might have over her. A man who was her answer to the perfect mate, but completely unsuitable, as well as completely unattainable.

Captain Gavin MacManus!

CHAPTER
NINE

THE brief calm was over. The *Atlanta* was making heavy weather again and passengers bound for the ultimate destination—New York—were informed that their arrival would be two days later than scheduled, since the engines must be checked over in Halifax, at the end of their trial run.

Many received this news with anger and indignation— the rescue of the Russian emigrants was to blame. The Captain's bulletin was not very popular with the crew either, especially stewards and chefs. As for the Captain himself, he had lost the bounty and what else could he lose but his command?

He considered that small measure to weigh against the survival of fifty human souls. Besides he believed that he could rely on Sir Joshua's kind heart. The ship-owner who had consistently come out on the side of the steerage passengers—and it was rumoured that the Wainwright Line had lost money by taking them across the Atlantic for a mere pittance—would be sympathetic to his Captain's behaviour regarding the survivors of the *Odessa*.

Simson looked at the Captain with new eyes. He had become a hero. 'A fine gentleman he is, Miss Faye. God bless him.'

Teddy was prepared to be philosophical. Time now mattered little to him. Eternally optimistic, he regarded the *Atlanta's* delayed arrival as two days' grace in which to persuade Faye to marry him. And her fortune was calculated to reinstate him completely with his irate parent, who would not be amused at having to meet yet another large gambling debt—acquired by his son on the *Atlanta's* lost speed-record!

As for Faye, since the discovery of her feelings for

Captain MacManus the sea had become her only reality. But daily she hoped—and longed—for a message on the telegraph machine from the Gaffer.

Believing her own fortunes could be little altered by the *Atlanta's* delays, she marvelled at the recent change in Simson. A new Simson, who seemed oblivious to the violent motion of the ship when she returned to the stateroom anxious to attend her mistress in any spare moment left to her.

A new Simson, thought Faye sadly, who was also a stranger. She had found her rightful niche in life. She no longer needed Faye or the Wainwrights.

'Sir Joshua was right all the time, Miss,' she reminded her beaming, 'It *is* a question of mind over matter. I reckon that now I'm so busy, my sickness seems trivial compared with the sufferings of these poor men.'

In response to an appeal from the Captain for any pieces of warm apparel for the refugees, Faye considered what else she could spare from her wardrobe. She regarded the resulting bundle with a wry smile. At least she had solved one problem: there was no need for extra closet space now.

She decided not to wait for the stewards' collection but to deliver her bundle of garments personally. Her main reason was curiosity; she wanted to see Simson in this new setting.

She packed as many as possible into the largest jacket, using the belt to contain them. With shawls and lighter garments slung over one shoulder she started off down the corridor. It was not an easy progress. The rocking movement of the ship caused her difficulty in keeping her feet, and within a few yards of Teddy's cabin door she considered calling upon his assistance. However, his door remained firmly closed and she decided that at this hour he would be ensconced in the smoking-room, that retreat of all the males in the ship.

Very well, she would go down to the hold alone, even if the journey, without Teddy or her spectacles, threatened to be a hazardous venture. Pride overcame prudence. She told herself that she knew the geography of the ship well by now. Besides, it was brilliantly lit by electricity. She observed through the portholes that there was a violent storm with flashes of lightning occasionally illuminating the sky. The quickest way would have been across the decks, but she winced from the darkness, the heavy rain and a slippery deck.

The safest way was to take the elevator to the lower decks and then descend by the stairs to Hold 3. All went well and, clutching her bundle, she was congratulating herself on her foresight and about to step out of the elevator when the lights went out.

Horrified, she pushed open the door, and not realising at first that the lights over the entire ship had failed, wandered along hoping to see some brightness at the end of the corridor. That was her first big mistake. She knew she was lost. She should never have left the elevator, she realised as she stumbled along what seemed like a narrow corridor in pitch darkness.

The whole effect was terrifying. She could find nothing on either hand but a smooth wall. She stopped and called for help, but no one came. The sensible thing would be to sit down in the darkness and wait for the lights to go on again or for someone to answer her call. But, she realised, sheer panic soon puts an end to sensible coherent thought. She was blind and lost. All she could hear was the heavy reverberation of the engines, the movement of the ship. As she stumbled along it seemed to grow darker, more airless, and as feelings of hysteria gripped her by the throat, at last she touched a smooth wall and, sighing with relief, traced the outline of a panelled door, and best of all, the door had a handle.

Thank heaven! Her held breath was a sob in her throat. On the other side there might be lights, people. She turned the handle, walked forward a few steps and even as she screamed, she was precipitated into thin air. For a moment, before the blackness rose to meet her with agonising pain, she thought she would never stop falling . . .

When the lights went on shortly afterwards, a steward noticed the open door and, seeing the still figure lying at the base of the steps, he alerted Captain MacManus.

Over the telegraph, the Captain had just received grave news concerning Sir Joshua and he had been on his way to Faye's stateroom. When he saw her lying there, his first thought was that she was dead.

What in heaven's name had she been doing down here? Then he saw the bundle of clothes. Was she once again defying his orders? Sending the steward for Dr Moore, he carried her gently to his own cabin which was nearer. Without knowing how badly she was hurt, he did not relish the prospect of carrying her back to her stateroom, meeting and alarming other passengers on the way.

When he laid her on the bed, her eyelids flickered open. She groaned. At least she was alive, he consoled himself that she had fallen only a few feet down the ladder. However, in the darkness that must have been a terrifying experience. Seeing him bending over her, she struggled to sit up. He kept his arms about her:

'Are you hurt?'

Wincing, she stretched out her arms, her legs. 'No-o—at least, I don't think so.'

Gently he touched her forehead and she flinched, following his hand. 'You have the beginnings of a nasty bruise—you must have come in violent contact with the steps when you fell. Here,' he took a towel and cold water and dabbed her forehead. 'Is that better?'

It was. 'I've asked for Dr Moore to come and take a look at you.'

'Please—that isn't necessary.' She stood up, swung her legs off the bed, and walked a few paces. 'There—you see—I'm fine now, really.'

'You were unconscious for some time.'

'When did the electricity go on again?'

He told her, and that the fuse had been caused by the storm. 'Repairs took the best part of a half-hour.' She looked at him sharply, feeling that suddenly exasperation had taken over from concern. Would this wretched girl never learn?

'I'll see you back to your stateroom. Your maid will take care of you—'

Faye shook her head. 'She isn't there, Captain. She's in sick bay—'

'I had no idea she was ill—'

'She isn't ill. She is helping your doctor nurse the Russian seamen.'

'She's *what*?'

'You asked for volunteers, Captain,' she reminded him gently.

He sighed. 'She has gone with your permission, of course.'

'Of course, Captain. And Dr Moore's. Did you think she would go without it? She's a fully trained nurse, that was her profession before she came to Wainwrights.' Faye smiled wryly. 'When I was a baby—I can't remember a time in my life without her. But I think she must always have had a hankering to return, once I grew up—somehow she never got around to broaching the subject. Besides, we were always so happy. I needed her, you see, especially with Grandfather away at sea so often.'

And a very bleak vision presented itself before Gavin MacManus of a girl without parents, in a great empty house, without companionship of her own age, with no one but her maid. He shuddered and remembered his own crowded childhood, poor but undoubtedly happy.

'You know you shouldn't have been wandering about the ship,' he chided her gently.

When she didn't reply he continued: 'You could have asked the steward to deliver those for you,' he pointed to the absurd belted bundle on the floor.

'It was just an impulse—I'm sorry to have caused so much trouble. At least there will be no need for those extra closets I requested, now.'

'I did give an order about collection, Miss Wainwright, did it not reach you?' He sounded very stern and Faye smiled wanly into that unyielding face.

'I wanted to see my maid—how she was getting along—and if I could do anything to help.'

The Captain gave a despairing shrug. What was the use of making rules when this girl either made her own, or interpreted everything that was said in a way to suit her impulses, as she called them. Useless to argue with her. Thank heaven he hadn't a shipful of rich and forceful young misses.

'You see, the elevator had already stopped when the lights went out,' she explained. 'Fortunately we were on floor level, but—' she shuddered—'I hadn't the slightest idea which way to go, except that I didn't want to stay in that beastly cage until the lights went on again. I have this thing about—about being trapped in the dark, so I decided to take a chance on finding my way—'

'And you almost found yourself with a broken neck,' snapped the Captain, his patience exhausted. 'Well, since you are still in one piece, I'll escort you safely back, in case you fall into some other misadventures. And I think we'll have your maid summoned back to take care of you for a while.'

Faye looked around. 'I've been thinking—I recognise this cabin, don't I? It is my grandfather's.'

His face expressionless, he nodded. Smiling, she touched the worn leather chair. 'I remember it so well—the hours we sat here together—' she sniffed the air. 'Do you know, I can almost still smell his pipe, the very strong tobacco he loved. How strange! It's—it's as if he is here with us.' She sighed, and added almost to herself, 'I wish he was.'

The Captain looked at her. He ought to tell her—this moment. He felt it too, the old man's presence—

'Miss Wainwright—there is something—'

But the words remained unsaid. She had her hand on the door when suddenly her eyes closed. Her head slipped forward and he caught her as she fell. Like a rag doll she lay limply against him. Even as he gathered her into his arms, her eyes flickered open.

'Phew—that was nasty. For a girl who has never fainted in her entire life, I'm doing rather well,' she added with a shaky laugh. And touching the growing bruise on her forehead, she winced.

'We'll get Dr Moore to take a look at you.'

'A good idea.' He still had his arms around her and she did a surprising thing. She stood on tiptoe and kissed his cheek. 'Thank you, Captain for rescuing me. I'm sorry for being such a nuisance.'

A nuisance—this enchanting creature whose warmth spread into his loneliness like sunshine through a dark wood? He felt the life-fires leap within him and his lips sought hers in a gentle kiss, unavoidable and natural as drawing breath. She did not flinch away from him, but returned his kiss. With a small sigh of pleasure, her arms reached up around his neck—

The rapidly approaching footsteps belonged in another world and Captain MacManus was merely supporting Miss Wainwright, who had suffered an accident, when Dr Moore entered. Together they helped her back to her stateroom.

The Captain stayed while the doctor examined her injuries and pronounced her fit and well apart from 'that bash on your forehead'.

'Plenty of rest—take things easy for the next day or two.' When Faye protested, he added: 'Could be delayed concussion—spells of dizziness, headaches. Your maid can call me at any time—'

'I can call you myself, Doctor, I don't want Simson wasting her time with me—not when she has patients who need her.'

Dr Moore grinned. 'I shall certainly miss my new nurse. She's one in a thousand, an absolute marvel. I don't know how I would have managed without her services. She tells me she hasn't nursed for twenty years—is that right? Well, she's born to it—and there are quite a few among those poor devils down below who may thank her that they are still alive.'

'Perhaps the *Atlanta* should have a resident nurse, doctor. I'll mention it to my grandfather, if you like.'

'In normal circumstances, it isn't necessary, Miss Wainwright. The stewards have rudimentary first aid training, the passengers have maids and valets—in first class anyway. Truth to tell, there's little need even for a doctor's services on such a short voyage—nothing to do mostly but issue seasickness pills or look at a child's sore throat. Thank God we don't get an emergency like shipwrecked emigrants every voyage.'

Simson returned promptly, shocked by her mistress's misadventure. Examining the bruised forehead with expert fingers, she endorsed the doctor's opinion that, although there was no evident damage, there could be delayed concussion.

'My poor wee lamb,' she said, 'you were knocked out cold, just like a boxer in the ring—one swift blow! I don't think it's anything a good rest won't cure, but you must do exactly that—rest.'

When Faye insisted she should return to her patients, Simmy said; 'No, they've been bedded down for the night. If anything serious happens, the doctor knows where to find me. So no more arguing, miss—I'm staying here. And you are going to bed, right now.'

As the maid prepared her for retiring, Faye said: 'Dr Moore is delighted with your help, he says you're a born nurse.'

Simson beamed. 'I love it. Do you know, Miss Faye, I can't remember when I've been happier, or enjoyed myself so much. Enjoyed, now that's a terrible word to use about nursing poor sick and injured folk. What I really mean is I feel so useful—and satisfied.' She paused. 'Oh, miss, not that I haven't been happy—and useful, I hope, to you all these years.'

'I know exactly what you mean, Simmy dear, there's no need to feel that an apology is needed. Looking after me—'

'Has been wonderful, Miss Faye. You know that.' She took the girl's slim hands into her strong grasp.

'But I can't go on being a helpless—girl—for ever, the way you and the Gaffer have kept me. You've been so good, both of you, always there to protect me, never allowing me to do anything for myself. But now—' she bit her lip, 'I feel that someday, perhaps very soon, I'll have my own responsibilities.'

Simson regarded her eagerly. 'Does this mean, Miss, what I think it means?' she began hopefully.

Faye frowned and then laughed at Simson's knowing glance. 'That I may get married?'

'Oh yes, miss.'

'Well, I hope so—one day.'

'And that not too far off?' whispered the maid.

Faye smiled and said no more.

As she had suspected from the passengers on the *Atlanta,* romance was not only for the young and love could last a whole life long. Love—was it for her only an illusion—a dream? She could not be quite sure where fantasy and reality met.

She was *almost* sure that Captain MacManus had been kissing her when Dr Moore appeared! Now remembering how faint and giddy was her condition at that time, she *wondered* . . .

The ill-tidings that Captain MacManus had been on his way to deliver to Faye when he had been forestalled by the steward's discovery of her lying injured by her fall, now had to wait a little longer.

He had already decided it would be folly—and utter cruelty—to inflict this grave news upon her in her present state of shock. When he told Dr Moore, the latter said sternly:

'Keep it until morning, if she's fit enough by then. If not—' he shrugged. 'There's nothing she can do until we reach Halifax at the earliest. But what about the *Atlanta,* Captain? Do we fly her flag at half-mast?'

'No, we don't.' The Captain showed him the package he had newly opened. 'Sir Joshua gave me these before we left. He said: "Open these—my orders—only if the worst happens." I thought little of it at the time, but when I heard over the telegraph that Sir Joshua had died—on the eve of going into hospital—I realised that he must have had a very strong suspicion about what lay ahead. There is a letter for Miss Wainwright, and this one contains my orders.'

These were plain. The Captain was not to make public Sir Joshua's death until the voyage was at an end, since the news might cast a blight over the carefree happy atmosphere that Sir Joshua was so proud to maintain on board his ship. In the event of the speed-record being broken, news of his death was in no way to influence the natural jubilation among the crew and extra rum rations were to be issued all round. The only concession to mourning was to be the draping in black silk of his portrait on the landing of the grand staircase. 'No others,' the letter concluded, 'since many passengers are old friends who have travelled regularly through the years, it is my wish that they retain a cheerful memory of their old Captain and, as always, I wish all friends of the Wainwright Line, old and new, to enjoy every moment of their voyage on the *Atlanta*.'

'I don't envy you, Captain,' said the doctor, 'having to break this piece of news to the girl. Be as gentle as you can.'

CHAPTER
TEN

Faye had been taking things quietly as Dr Moore ordered. She had not been prepared for Teddy's reaction to the accident. He made no end of a fuss, scowling and muttering that someone should be sued for the failure of the electricity and that damned door.

'May I remind you that my grandfather, as owner, would be legally responsible,' said Faye sweetly. 'Perhaps you have in mind to start proceedings against *him*.'

'I didn't mean the Gaffer—you know that. It wasn't *his* fault,' said Teddy.

'You can't sue for an act of God, Teddy dear. So do shut up.' His grumbling made her head ache. 'Besides I was only knocked out—I'm not permanently damaged.'

'All the same—'

Faye found Teddy's presence very tiresome that afternoon. She had another reason for disquiet. She was not in the least keen on receiving him in her stateroom without Simson as chaperon, especially as she had constantly to evade his straying hands and determined embraces. Even for one in the best of health and spirits, it would be trying indeed, but in her weakened state she could hardly bear that daily proposal of marriage, which to his mind made his advances honourable!

Teddy regarded himself firmly as her suitor and reproached her frequently that she *would* love him, if only she would learn to relax and let human nature take over.

'You're far too prim and prissy, that's what. Where's the harm in a little kissing and cuddling, for heaven's sake?—there's plenty of that going on all over the ship. Why can't we have a little fun—why are you so cold and unyielding?'

As she shrugged away from him once again, Faye

smiled secretly as she remembered the real woman who lurked in the depths of her being was a wild, passionate and completely abandoned creature who might have terrified Teddy Haversham!

Such were her thoughts when Captain MacManus arrived. He regarded her solemnly as he stood in the doorway and enquired after her health. Assuring him of her complete recovery she added; 'I do hope you haven't come to lecture me again, Captain. I have had quite enough of that today—'

In answer he came in quickly and took her hands. 'If that were my duty only, I would be glad indeed. Please—' he looked around, 'may we sit down?'

'Of course.' Puzzled, she let him lead her to the sofa.

'Faye, I have bad news—from Southampton—'

'Grandfather—he's worse—'

The Captain shook his head and handed her the letter. The words in the Gaffer's bold handwriting leaped out at her:

'To my beloved granddaughter Faye Wainwright, in the event of my death—'

Death.

'Oh no—no—please tell me it isn't that—please—not the Gaffer—*no*—'

The Captain took her hands and held them firmly. 'Last night—the message came through—'

'Then why didn't you tell me—why wait all this time?'

'Because of Dr Moore's strict orders that you must have a good night's rest. Oh, forgive me, Faye—forgive me.'

She began to sob hysterically and he gathered her into his arms. She made no resistance but clung to him like a hurt and frightened child. For how long he held her so, he had no idea. Apart from his agony for her sorrow, he realised how much he wanted her, how greatly he loved holding her so close.

Her hair smelt warm and feminine, a delicate rose perfume clung about her in an intoxicating aura, as if in her remote world, summer was eternal. Cradling her gently, he said:

'Hush—there, there, *mo gràdh*',' using the Gaelic

words as he might to a child, and at the same time wondering with compassion how this frail sheltered creature was going to face the future, now that the life always so organised had collapsed at its very foundations. Was she strong enough to survive, so young and vulnerable, without her grandfather's vigorous presence and advice?

At last her tears ceased and, with an exhausted sigh, she moved away from him. How beautiful she was in tragedy, he thought. Such tears, such anguish merely enhanced her loveliness. She had picked up the letter from her grandfather and thrust it into his hands.

'Please read it to me.'

'Are you sure?'

'Yes.'

'Very well.' The letter was written in the simplest of terms. It told Faye that all the arrangements had been made for her future and were in the capable hands of Warren Schroeder, Sir Joshua's oldest friend. Warren Schroeder had volunteered to act as trustee for her until she came of age on her birthday next June, unless she married before that date, when such matters would become the responsibility of her husband. The Captain was puzzled for there was no mention of the Wainwright Line nor of the estate at Southampton. Faye did not seem to notice these omissions, so he decided that Mr Schroeder would be informing her. The letter ended abruptly: 'Forgive me, my darling girl. There are no words I can say that will not add to your grief. I wish I could spare you this pain and the pain of the future. Remember that I watch over you. Remember that I love you, always.'

As he read the words, she stopped pacing the floor, wringing her hands. 'Again,' she whispered. 'That part—again.'

'Remember that I love you always.'

As if the word 'love' was a magic key to unlock their hearts, he put down the letter and, rapidly covering the space between them, stood before her. She gave a single stricken cry, and flung herself into his arms, still sobbing, but this time she clung around his neck, her face wet with tears. She kissed his cheek. He stroked back her hair and, taking her face in his hands, gently turned her chin towards him. His lips found hers and he began to kiss her. At first, with the gentle compassion of sympathy, quite unlike that first time, when he was angry with her on the bridge. Then, as if the thought of that other time communicated itself to him, his kisses changed and she was responding.

Their lips fused together as arms tightened, bodies drew close, closer . . . They clung together, moaning a little as they swayed in the tumultuous passion which had them in its growing fever.

Where would it end, thought Faye. Please, God, don't let it ever end—

'Listen.' He had stopped kissing her, her lips felt cold without his warm mouth.

'It's nothing,' she said and tightening her hold about his neck, lifted her mouth to his.

'It's—the door. Someone at the door.' He pushed her aside, straightened his tie, ran a hand through the heavy black hair which was unrulier than either passengers or crew had ever seen it.

Faye's senses were reeling. Oh dear God, to let this moment be spoiled like this . . .

'Miss, miss? Open the door, oh do please, Miss Faye.'

Thank heaven it was Simmy and not Teddy—if she could be thankful for anything—

'Just a moment, Simmy.' She glanced in the mirror, tucked in a strand of hair, saw that not only had she a bruise on her forehead but her chin was also reddening, her lip swollen. She looked at Captain MacManus, he nodded briskly and she marvelled at his calm. He reached the door ahead of her and before she turned the lock, he ran a gentle finger down the line of her cheek.

'Saved by the bell,' he murmured, his mouth twitching in mockery.

Simson was plainly taken aback to see Captain MacManus with Faye at his side. Faye felt certain they both looked guilty, and she moved away from the Captain more hurriedly than was necessary.

'Oh, Miss, miss—I've just heard the terrible news.

The doctor said I was to come to you right away—' She paused, looked from one to the other.

The Captain cleared his throat. 'I have just broken the news to Miss Wainwright.'

Faye looked at him: his stern and unyielding face gave nothing away. Tall and correct; immaculate as always, no one could ever imagine that a few moments ago they had been locked in a lovers' embrace. Lovers? Could this be the same man, the wild and passionate creature who lurked behind the handsome uniform, the gold braid?

'Oh, miss,' said Simmy and held out her arms. Faye went to her gladly, sobbing. Over her head, Captain MacManus was aware of the maid's reproachful face.

How much did she guess, he wondered as bowing he said softly: 'Take care of her, she took it very badly. Excuse me.'

Faye would see no one.

'Not even Mr Teddy, miss?' Simson sounded surprised.

Faye shook her head. Teddy least of all, she thought. She did not want him holding her in his arms. She did not want his too-ready shoulder to cry on, his ready kisses.

Simson was worried. The lass's tears had ceased, but she sat in a corner of the stateroom, against the wall, as if she would shrink into shelter like a hurt animal.

'Here, Miss Faye, your bed is all ready. Now drink this—it'll help to make you sleep. You'll feel better by morning.'

Wordlessly she obeyed, allowed Simson to lead her into the bedroom and prepare her for bed, like a rag doll. Soon she was asleep. Simson reckoned that the sedative would last at least three hours in its effects, as she closed the door quietly and stole down to check on her patients in the sick bay. There were three men still fighting for life—at least with Halifax on the horizon tomorrow, they might survive if by then, they were not beyond hospital treatment.

When she returned, Faye still slept. In the morning, she awoke briefly, but showed no desire to leave her bed. She drank the cup of tea Simson offered, refused to eat, and once again sunk into a deep sleep.

The maid stayed by her side, apart from interruptions caused by Mr Teddy's constant appearance at the door. He had heard the news, longed to commiserate with his beloved girl. Simson was sorry for him.

That evening after the dinner hour, she had to go down to change dressings on the injured men. She told the Steward to keep a sharp lookout in case Miss Faye's bell rang.

Faye heard the door close on the maid, and then she got out of bed. She felt like someone living in a nightmare from which there was no possible awakening, for she now saw clearly that last parting with Grandfather, reliving it over and over in her mind. He had known he was dying, known that they would never meet again. If she could be grateful for anything, it was that he had died in his own bed at Wainwrights.

There was a gentle rap on the door. Faye listened, realised it was not Teddy, whose forceful summons she recognised with dread these days.

Probably just the Steward. 'Who is it?' she asked
'Captain MacManus.'

She opened the door and he regarded her anxiously. 'I was worried about you, I realised that you would not be appearing at dinner. Your grandfather wished the passengers to be kept in ignorance, so Mr Haversham gave the excuse that you had a chill.'

She looked at him fixedly, her expression like that of a sleep-walker. 'Do come in.'

When she closed the door, he said: 'I've been unable to get you out of my mind—all day I've thought of you.'

She was amazed at such a frank confession, for whenever she had thought of the Gaffer, the Captain's was the image that swam before her eyes and refused to be banished.

'You see, Faye, I also loved Sir Joshua. He was like a father to me—there was nothing on God's earth I would not have done for him.' He paused, shook his head. 'I can't believe that such a good, kind, *dynamic* man, has gone from this earth—'

He brushed a hand across his eyes and the sight moved Faye more than any words.

'I can't believe it either. *I can't.* Never to see him—never to have him waiting to welcome me home. Home! Oh dear God—Wainwrights without him. I can't bear it—'

Suddenly she began to cry. Sobs racked her slight body and Gavin MacManus held out his hands.

'I'm sorry,' she said 'I'm sorry—'

He waited no longer. He closed the little space between them and gathered her into his arms. Head buried on his shoulder, she wept unrestrainedly, while he stroked her hair, murmured to her the Gaelic words which for him were so much easier and more meaningful than English could ever be.

As if she listened and was consoled, her tears ceased. She raised her face to his, touched his cheek with a gentle exploratory hand. Then, suddenly, her lips fluttered against his chin. Found his mouth—

This time there was no delay between them. The time was past for gentle exploration, for they both knew the way, the path had already been discovered and the ecstasy it held waited still.

Lips were one thing, but bodies too demanded something more than kisses. His arms dropped to her waist, outlined the slender frame from breast to waist, and on—

She made no resistance, only a gentle moan. Then a whisper: 'Hold me—hold me—'

A savage fury possessed him now, a hunger not to be denied. He lifted her in his arms and carried her to the bed, his hands tore at the neck of her robe, his lips covered her slender neck with kisses. Hands free now, busily released her from the confining garment. Soon she would be loved—loved at last—

But the moment never came.

She opened her eyes, aware that he held her no longer. She looked up, sweetly held out her arms.

He shook his head. 'No. No.'

'Why not—in God's name, why not—'

Again he shook his head. How could he explain that at

that last moment, that point of no return, a face had come between him and the lovely girl on the bed beside him. A beloved face, reproachful and tearful, as if to remind him of another girl like the one before him, a girl who also came from a rich and powerful family, whose life had been utterly destroyed by just such a moment as this. A moment of loving, not wisely but too well. How could he tell her of the series of pictures which fled through his mind, like a drowning man's vision: of the love that consumed that other girl, the child born of that forbidden night of love, the forced marriage, the family who spurned her afterwards. And then the rest of her life in exile and poverty, regretting the wild blood, the impulse that defied convention, but was not strong enough to survive the long bitter lawsuits which turned passion into degradation and love into ashes.

No. Before such a bitter irony, he could not take this girl, even in love, as he now knew was the case. Even in lust, with the desire for revenge, he could not.

'Please dress yourself, someone might come in.'

She heard the cold harsh words and stared at him unbelieving, and he turned from the betrayal blazing in her eyes.

'You've done the buttons up wrongly,' he said dully. As he went over to her, she screamed:

'Keep away from me—keep away—'

'Faye—'

'Don't touch me.'

'Faye, my darling, *mo gradh*—'

'I am not your darling—now or ever—'

'Faye, listen to me.' He put his hand on her arm, and she sprang away from him, as if the touch was violation.

'You must listen—let me explain.'

'There is nothing to explain.'

'But there is. If I were free to love you—'

'*No* excuses, for God's sake, spare me that. I don't want your reasons—'

'Faye, it isn't—'

'I don't care what it is or isn't—your reasons don't interest me.' She squared her shoulders facing him.

'You *will* listen.' He came forward, seized her roughly

and was rewarded by her swinging away from him. His pursuit was followed by a stinging blow across his face. He reeled back, astonished.

She had reached the door, opened it. 'I hate you, Captain MacManus—kindly leave this room immediately—'

'But—'

'And do not ever address me again. Do I make myself quite clear? I never wish to speak to you again.'

She turned away and when she looked round the room was empty. Empty like her heart, a heart turned to stone.

For Captain Gavin MacManus, the story was not quite at an end. Later that evening, still considerably shaken by his disastrous encounter with Faye, he received an imperious summons: The Hon Edward Haversham wished to see him in his cabin immediately.

As the Captain made his way to first-class his thoughts were very uneasy. What on earth did Haversham want? As he waited outside the door, for a moment he wondered guiltily if Faye had rushed to the young man with a tale of rape. And as the voice inside called 'Enter' he wondered if he would find himself staring down the barrel of a pistol or being offered merely the gentleman's alternative of 'putting up his fists'.

He was somewhat surprised to find the Earl's son in excellent humour, to the extent of offering him a drink and a cigar. Wondering, the Captain accepted both and took a seat opposite. Regarding Haversham narrowly through the smoke, he wondered if he had misjudged him. What had happened to replace Haversham's normally rude or chilly attitude with that air of suppressed excitement? The Captain was shrewdly aware that Teddy Haversham would not readily forgive an affront to his dignity, and being called an 'idiotic child' had been an unwise remark.

'You must be wondering why I asked you here, Captain,' said Haversham, his face suddenly grave. 'As I expect you know, we are intensely grieved at the news of

Miss Wainwright's sad loss. I am sure the crew of the *Atlanta* and the passengers who knew and travelled with Sir Joshua will find him irreplaceable.'

If Captain MacManus received the gentle sneer at his own capabilities, he gave no sign of it.

'For Miss Wainwright and myself, however, this melancholy event is not without significance,' Haversham continued, 'Miss Wainwright is now alone in the world and once the period of mourning is over, I hope to have the honour of making her my wife. However, as she has no legal guardian—'

Captain MacManus regarded him sharply. Was he not aware that the American millionaire, Warren Schroeder, had been appointed by Sir Joshua in that capacity?

'As my—er, suit—had Sir Joshua's full approval and blessing, and as Miss Wainwright and I have—er, well,' he permitted himself to smirk before continuing, 'shall we say, grown close, during the voyage.' He paused but was disappointed if he expected any other reaction from the Captain but polite inscrutability. 'The point that concerns you, Captain, is a question' Fingertips pressed together he smiled and waited.

'Your question is, sir?' asked Captain MacManus slowly.

'Whether you have powers to perform the marriage ceremony between Miss Wainwright and myself.'

The Captain shook his head. 'That is not within the powers of the master of any British vessel. I am afraid you must wait until we reach our destination.'

'*Damn*!' Haversham stood up scowling and indicated that the interview was at an end. As the Captain reached the door, he recovered himself enough to add: 'My fiancée will be extremely disappointed with this piece of news. She has a romantic turn of nature and a shipboard marriage would greatly appeal to her.'

Captain MacManus said nothing. He merely bowed and closed the door. So that was it, he decided grimly. Miss Faye Wainwright *had* been playing a game with him, the stakes probably marriage to Haversham. She had been endeavouring for reasons best known to herself to make the Earl's son jealous!

And Captain MacManus could have cheerfully kicked himself for his folly. What a fool he had been, such a willing and devoted pawn in that little game of grief and inconsolable loss.

It would never happen again. He'd see to that.

His heart no longer ached quite so wretchedly as he returned to the cold and lonely bridge. He had learned his lesson and he owed his survival to learning fast. He never made the same mistake twice. And the sour, bitter taste of rejection would end all his present fantasies about the sad and beautiful Miss Faye Wainwright.

CHAPTER
ELEVEN

THE *Atlanta* entered the port of Halifax, Nova Scotia, early the following morning. Here she would dock briefly, set ashore the Russian emigrants and take on passengers bound for New York.

Their arrival was considerably overdue and Captain MacManus had little time to grieve over his lost bounty or, more particularly, Faye Wainwright, and their last disastrous encounter. He was grateful as the pilot boat sped across to guide them into harbour that the passage was still clear of ice, although the ships anchored alongside glistened like sugar cakes under frost.

After customs and quarantine clearance, the Russians trudged through the brown slush of melting snow. They were a pathetic sight in their ill-assorted garments, their breath steaming in the icy air.

The Captain was eager to be under way again, for the sky had an ominously leaden look. He hoped to arrive in New York ahead of winter conditions which were already prevalent in this more northern port.

The Scottish engineer, Peter Bain, who had acted as the Russians' interpreter for the last time told the Captain of the survivors' heartfelt gratitude, and, that if the seriously injured seamen lived, they would owe their lives to the Captain of the *Atlanta*, the doctor, and Miss Simson, who had so devotedly nursed them.

'One more thing, Captain—a favour. I should like to remain aboard until we reach New York. I've changed my mind about Canada—especially as my life with the Russians is finished. I'm considering going back to Scotland—ach, it's been a fair long time. Mind you, Captain, I haven't a brass cent to pay my way, but perhaps I can make myself useful during the next two days—'

The Captain put a hand on his shoulder. 'Don't even

think about that. You're more than welcome to stay with us. How's the leg?'

'Not bad. At least I still have two legs—which is more than I might have done had it not been for Miss Simson. I can't tell you how grateful I am—and the crew of the *Odessa* and their families too.' He paused. 'We all know what these delays meant to you—the speed record and all—'

'I don't give a damn about that!'

But he did. He had failed Sir Joshua and his faith in the new engines. He groaned. What kind of a man was he turning into these days? He saw Simson talking to Bain by the ship's rail. How cheerful and friendly they seemed together, always sharing a joke. He sighed. Why in heaven's name could Faye not have been maid instead of mistress? He smiled tenderly at such a fantasy. How happy they would have been, she proud to be a Captain's wife, he with his thousand pounds and the prospect of a glorious future together.

But Faye Wainwright was not the maid. Nor had he the slightest hope of any thousand pounds. And what was more, Faye was all set to marry Teddy Haversham. He thought of her abandoned behaviour, trying to interpret the meaning of those kisses. No doubt she was the kind of rich girl he had heard about, 'slumming' as the wealthy did in the poor districts of London, and having one last fling with the rough and passionate wooing of a man she considered beneath her.

The thought stung. He shuddered away from memory. Let her marry Haversham. Doubtless they deserved each other.

Faye would have been surprised indeed had she known of Teddy's request for a shipboard wedding. She knew that Captain MacManus could never be hers, that there were too many barriers of class and custom to be wrenched down between them. She also knew, in her heart of hearts, that Teddy was ideally suited by birth and that the Gaffer would have been delighted since the Earl's son had long been his choice for her.

The world in which she lived too, would smile its

approval—everyone would be pleased, Simmy most of all. There was only one snag. She did not love him. She was still in love with Gavin MacManus, a realisation which brought her only bitter anguish.

She knew from her close friends' experiences that there is one certain way to forget a man, and that is to replace him swiftly by another.

Yes, there were excellent reasons for marrying Teddy. But were loneliness and insecurity sufficient reasons? She sighed. If only marriage were a glorified 'friendship', but the idea of Teddy's wet kisses was intolerable. However, considering her behaviour with Captain MacManus, she was certainly in need of love and comfort of some kind to satisfy the thirst deep within her. She realised fearfully that her interlude with the Captain had touched hidden depths of passion in her being.

Perhaps Teddy would be able to reawaken those desires. Would she ever cease to blush as she remembered her furious dismissal of the Captain, and the events which led to it. She touched her bare flesh which still burned with the memory of his kisses and she hung her head in misery. What could he possibly think of her?

She remained in her cabin while the *Atlanta* docked at Halifax and did not emerge until the pilot boat had led them once more out of harbour and into the open sea.

Thank heaven, the Captain would be busily employed until they reached New York. There was no reason why they should meet again except in the brief formality of leave-taking, especially since she would, in mourning for her grandfather, remain in her stateroom. She guessed that this would also be a relief to the Captain and that his pride would keep him well away from her vicinity.

In New York, Warren Schroeder was saddened greatly by the tidings wired from Southampton. However, he was not only surprised but relieved that Sir Joshua had been spared the ordeal of hospital, and that he had closed his eyes for the last time in the peace and comfort of his own bed at Wainwrights.

Wainwrights. Warren felt the full impact of the news

for the first time. Wainwrights with its magnificent house and estate and the shipping line were now his. That such good fortune had been brought about by his old friend's death was a piece of irony. However, he was not a man to waste time in sentimental brooding and he set in motion the legal matters which would seal his ownership.

As for the girl—well, he had his own plans for her too. Meanwhile, he sent a cable of condolence to the *Atlanta* and in return received a message that the liner had been delayed, because of returning to search for Russian survivors from the *Odessa*.

Warren Schroeder was furious as he paced back and forth in his elegant Fifth Avenue house. What had that fool of a young Captain in mind? Didn't he realise that the speed-record had been at stake? He banged his fists together. My, how he would enjoy giving MacManus a piece of his mind—when he fired him—and told him that the bonus of one thousand pounds, which Sir Joshua had promised, would no longer be forthcoming. 'Get out of my office,' he would roar. Oh yes, he would enjoy that little scene.

His thoughts turned to his sister Dulcie. She would join the *Atlanta* and become Faye's chaperon in New York. Dulcie had a good sharp eye. She could be relied upon to spot any improvements necessary when the *Atlanta* and the lesser ships of the line became her brother's property.

The Schroeder Line! How imposing it sounded and for the first time that day Warren was soothed. He felt like purring instead of swearing, even though he had some difficulty in getting through to Halifax by telephone, to warn Dulcie on a very crackling line, that Sir Joshua had died.

'Be kind to that little girl,' he said. 'I imagine she's inconsolable right now.'

A few hours later, Dulcie Schroeder, who had resumed her maiden name after her divorce, walked up the gangway of the *Atlanta,* where Captain MacManus was waiting to welcome new arrivals aboard.

She was moving house, she explained sweetly, as he

eyed her considerable luggage being unloaded from several automobiles.

'We have ample room,' he said. 'Welcome aboard.'

The Captain was impressed by Miss Schroeder. An American Southern belle, a well-endowed brunette, with a husky sensual voice, whose smile was also an invitation.

A closer look over dinner that evening—to which he escorted her—revealed that she was older and less pretty than upon her first dazzling appearance and that her good looks owed much to the art of cosmetics and the possession of flatteringly-cut clothes, easily accessible to those of great wealth.

Approaching forty, Dulcie had been a celebrated hostess in Halifax, but she longed to return to Virginia after the stifling atmosphere which had pervaded her marriage. The fact that her ex-husband owned a Canadian bank did nothing to alleviate the boredom of their life together.

Philip's dynasty required the provision of an heir, but Dulcie had dreaded such a prospect. She was not in the least maternal—besides a child might spoil her perfect figure. She did everything she could secretly to prevent pregnancy taking place.

After ten years of marriage, utterly bored with Philip, she had scrutinised the ranks of their friends and acquaintances and had not found it hard discreetly to acquire a lover. When that deception proved easy, a second and third affair followed. Lovers were a new and exciting aspect to her life, backed by a husband who provided wealth, generosity and asked no awkward questions. However, she had not bargained for one discarded lover who spitefully informed Philip of his wife's infidelity. An outraged Philip, to whom she now confessed everything, declared their marriage at an end. Forgiveness was out of the question, had she even wanted a second chance. Speedily and tidily, he gave her grounds for a divorce, but refused to give her as large a financial settlement as she craved.

Thank God for a brother like Warren and the prospect of a life in Virginia away from the scandal of it all. At least she was free and she wished for no other foray into the boredom of matrimony. However, this did not stop her regarding every attractive man as a potential lover . . .

She regarded Captain MacManus with considerable approval. She saw a handsome, well set-up man, and she found her mind racing ahead. Certainly an interesting prospect for a little dalliance; she liked the brooding dark glance, the silent power and restraint suggesting hidden fires that she was anxious now to light.

Captain MacManus, for his part, found her extremely attractive. She was exactly the kind of voluptuous woman he liked—Faye Wainwright had been a brief and notable exception to his usual type of womanly beauty . . . He was a little disappointed when she excused herself from the dinner table to call upon Miss Faye Wainwright. The fact that they were acquainted, that she was sister of the Warren Schroeder mentioned in Sir Joshua's letter, caused him a qualm of uneasiness.

In the stateroom, Faye wept anew as Dulcie offered her condolences. 'My dear Miss Wainwright, as you know my brother Warren was very close to Sir Joshua. And so your loss is ours, my dear. My brother has asked me to convey to you not only his sympathy but also to tell you that he—no—*we* will do everything in our power to make you welcome to our little home—'

Faye dried her tears. 'You are so very kind. But in the circumstances, I feel I must return to Wainwrights immediately.' At Dulcie's shocked exclamation, she smiled pathetically. 'Oh yes, I realise I shall be too late for the funeral, but I must arrange a memorial service. There is so much to do, I am quite at a loss where to begin.' She looked sadly at the one black dress from her wardrobe. 'You must forgive me for not being in full mourning. I have only this—'

Dulcie took her hands. 'My dear, we will get you suitable apparel in New York.'

'Perhaps your brother would be so kind as to book me a passage on the next ship for Southampton.'

'The *Atlanta* will be returning immediately—'

'No!' Faye's voice was so sharp that Dulcie stared at her. 'I mean—I wish to return on some other ship than this one—now—'

Of course, thought Dulcie, all those memories of her grandfather. 'I understand.'

Faye looked away. How could this kind woman understand her real reason, that she could not endure to return on any ship with Captain Gavin MacManus?

Faye could not delay her encounter with Teddy for ever. He had to be seen and he insisted that they discuss the future. He would return to Southampton with her—he refused to take no for an answer. He had rights—

Silently she handed him the letter from Sir Joshua.

'You have no rights, Teddy, not until I accept your proposal.'

Teddy laid the letter aside. 'You might as well do so, Faye; it's a bleak and lonely prospect at Wainwrights. I can help you through the next months—and the Pater will be delighted. Besides we can get married in New York, right away.' He paused. 'In fact, I *had* thought the Captain could marry us aboard the *Atlanta*. Now he tells me it isn't within his powers—'

'When did you ask him that?' she demanded sharply.

'The evening after the news came through.'

That *same* evening—oh dear God, what must he have thought of her?

By convention, bereavement demanded seclusion. And Faye had little desire to see anyone, least of all Teddy. She found it difficult to express such feelings, especially as Simson, who had returned to devote herself to her mistress once more, was definitely Teddy's ally.

Reluctantly, Faye agreed that they should dine together in her stateroom, with Simson present.

'What are your future plans?' she asked him and, observing his hurt expression, added hastily: 'Well, before we met here, were you not planning to go to a copper mine in Arizona?'

He shrugged indifferently. 'For a start—I suppose so.'

'It sounds like an excellent idea.'

'But—'

'Teddy, whatever is decided between us, eventually, I

cannot get married in New York—so there!'

'Why ever not?'

'Because it's too soon after the Gaffer—it would look as if we were being very hasty—had something to be ashamed of—'

'What an imagination you have, old girl.' Then he added tenderly. 'Is that your only objection?' And without waiting for her reply, he continued: 'Is it to be a white wedding at St Margaret's with a reception at the Savoy?'

She smiled. 'Grandfather would have wanted something like that.'

At her sudden sad face, Teddy said: 'I can't wait to tell the Pater—when you say yes, he'll be over the moon. And we can spend Christmas with the family at Darleigh. You'll love them.'

Teddy felt that fortune had smiled upon him at last. Pity he couldn't persuade Faye to the New York marriage though, since in the normal way she couldn't be expected to marry until she was out of mourning—at least another six months. Teddy considered that prospect gloomily. He favoured 'a bird in the hand' at any time and, a man of many clichés, he felt that by not clinching the deal he was losing the slight advantage he had gained. Besides, if he went to Arizona with their relationship in such delicate condition, he might lose her for ever.

It was not a comfortable evening. Teddy's reproaches became monotonous and Faye decided that he must be stone deaf, for he listened to nothing he did not wish to hear. It was as if he believed that he could wear down her resistance with a mixture of bullying and cajoling.

She was greatly relieved when another visitor appeared.

Dulcie Schroeder, radiant in purple velvet, daringly cut to show her magnificent bosom to best advantage, had called to enquire after Faye, whom she had not visited that day. She expressed anxiety and concern, took Faye in a warm embrace, and was very impressed to learn that the handsome young man sitting opposite was an Earl's son. He had the same highly-bred English look as Faye, she decided, and looked every inch an aristo-crat, inbred through many generations.

Teddy Haversham on his part, was so impressed by Dulcie's flamboyant looks that he failed to notice her talk centred almost entirely upon Captain Mac-Manus.

'Yes indeed, I sat next to him at dinner—his special guest,' she said proudly. 'A delightful table companion—so gallant. And then we danced, well, every dance, except for his boring duty ones with the older ladies. What a superb dancer the man is! Gee, my feet are aching, but not from any ill-use on his part, I assure you. I haven't danced as much in years. I guess I'll sleep without rocking tonight. Your Captain,' she said smiling at Faye who winced at the word 'Your', '—is great. We had a lovely talk all through dinner. He told me all about this darling island he comes from, 'way in the west of Scotland, with a cute wee castle overlooking the head-land—been there since the sixteenth century. Just im-agine, that old, and still lived in—'

Faye was amazed to learn of this new version of Gavin MacManus.

'And he taught me some words in his own language, Gaelic—*the* Gaelic, he calls it. I can't recall the greet-ing—oh damn, my memory is terrible.' She giggled, smiling lazily as if some mental image pleased her greatly. 'He is quite a man, your Captain,' she sighed.

From amazement, Faye slid into darkest depression. Imagine Dulcie learning so many things about the enigmatic Captain which he had never vouchsafed to her. She realised she knew nothing of Gavin MacManus, except that he was physically attractive to her and kissed remarkably well.

She regarded Dulcie thoughtfully. Obviously Warren Schroeder's divorced sister was very taken with the Captain. Perhaps such men found it easier to talk to experienced women of the world. Clearly the older woman had made tremendous—and enviable—pro-gress. And for the first time, Faye felt the piercing shaft of jealousy as she listened to this vitally vibrant rival who had now turned her attention to Teddy. In that moment,

Faye felt as if she had not been merely overlooked, but her presence forgotten entirely.

Her instincts were very near the truth. Teddy was most agreeably surprised by Dulcie Schroeder who, without shadow of a doubt, was the kind of woman he had always longed to meet, a woman who enjoyed her sex life to the full and asked nothing of a chap but the gratification of physical desires, an area about which Faye—that sweet child, God bless her—knew less than nothing.

Aware of Faye's concentrated gaze, which had a brooding quality, Teddy hastily withdrew from the conversation with Dulcie. After all, circumstances made it necessary for him to be content with Faye's celibate behaviour—she was still for him the goose that laid the golden egg. But he sometimes wondered what she would be like once they were married and the bedroom door was closed.

Talking to Faye, he eyed Dulcie surreptitiously. What a superb creature she was. Superb in every way, from her well-developed bosom, her rounded hips, to her deep-throated warm chuckle. She guessed a man's needs, he thought. And when he offered to escort her back to her cabin he was rewarded by a passionate embrace and a kiss that thrilled him. God, how enticing! It emboldened him to ask:

'Is that all I get—or is there more inside?' He nodded towards the still closed cabin door.

Smiling, she wagged a finger at him. 'You are a very naughty man, Teddy, to suggest such a thing.'

He kissed her again and she offered no resistance. When his hands strayed, she pushed him away saying: 'That is quite enough—for one night.'

'The aperitif, my dear?'

'Let's wait and see, shall we?' Her coquettish glance suggested delights in store as she closed the door. 'Goodnight—and sweet dreams.'

In her cabin, she waltzed dreamily to unheard music, much to the surprise of her maid who generally found her mistress very much out-of-sorts at the end of an evening, unless she was accompanied home by a lover.

Dulcie had reason for pleasurable thoughts. Both the *Atlanta's* Captain and an Earl's son were paying her gratifying attentions. Of the two, regretfully, she had to admit that she found the Captain the more attractive. He had an air of mystery, of powerful masculinity, which she found irresistible. She recalled those last moments between them before he went on duty.

A calm night, velvet black sky lit by a moon and stars, they had wandered together on to the deck.

'I think I ought to visit Miss Wainwright before I retire,' said Dulcie.

The Captain's face was hidden in the shadows but he was suddenly very still.

'However, I am not obliged to do so.' She touched his cheek. 'Perhaps we might make some arrangements of our own—for later, that is.'

He smiled at her. 'I have some arrangements, my dear Miss Schroeder. But alas, they are all concerned with the business of getting this ship to New York.' His arm about her shoulders tightened, as they returned under the awning towards the first-class cabins. 'Other more enticing matters, I am afraid, must wait.'

And Dulcie was still pondering on the hidden meaning—was it a promise and if so how could she bring about its fulfilment in only one day?—when she fell asleep.

CHAPTER
TWELVE

FAYE opened her eyes with considerable relief to the realisation that this was her last full day aboard the *Atlanta*. The world of the sea had undergone a subtle change since they left Halifax. They were now in the constant shadow of an unseen but great landmass, a continent which sheltered them from the cruelty of the ocean. Landfall signalled calmer weather and the return of the seabirds.

Traditionally on the last night there was a Grand Ball.

'Pity you can't go.' said Teddy.

'I have plenty to do,' Faye replied, a little hurt that he had not offered to relinquish the great occasion. For once—was it the prospect of the alluring Dulcie?—he did not grumble or protest that he must go alone.

'Sure you will be all right?' he said.

'Yes. I have lots of letters to write—to friends of Grandfather's.' Her dear friend Mary's husband—as a distant Wainwright cousin—would represent her at the funeral.

Later in the day, Teddy looked in again and seemed very eager to report Dulcie's activities.

'You should have seen her at luncheon. The Captain, my, he is taken with her. I would never have thought he was much of a lady's man, but the way he brightens at the sight of her! He seems absolutely fascinated, hanging upon her every word. I shouldn't be a bit surprised if they fall in love—'

'They hardly know each other.' Faye was surprised at the sharpness of her voice.

'That, my dear child, doesn't matter in the least. Love never takes the least account of time. Remember Romeo and Juliet? And talking of such matters—someone else is in love—the last person in the world I'd have thought would be troubled by Cupid's darts— Aren't you interested, old girl?'

Faye smiled at him tolerantly. 'Is it someone I know?'

'Someone very close to you.'

'Really?'

'You'll never believe when I tell you who it is. Have a guess.'

Faye found his guessing games irritating. She shook her head.

'Simson,' he said triumphantly. 'What do you think of that?'

'Simmy? I don't believe it.'

'You had better start trying, old girl. Since we left Halifax I've seen her walking up and down the deck with that Scotch engineer from the Russian ship. He's on crutches, of course, and she's helping him along.' He grinned. 'But it's all whispered conversation, very lovey-dovey—'

It was Faye's turn to laugh, with relief. 'You're imagining things, Teddy.'

He shook his head in mock sadness. 'That I am not. You'd better get used to the idea, Faye old girl, I think you are about to lose your Simmy.'

Lose Simmy! The idea had never entered Faye's wildest dreams. Never in all her thoughts had she envisaged a future without Simson, although she had promised herself that she would relinquish the maid to a noble life of nursing—when *she* married. At that time she hadn't known that she was also to lose Grandfather. To lose both of them . . . the whole structure and fabric of her life seemed to be dissolving before her eyes to reveal a bitter desolate future. She looked at Teddy. Perhaps he was right—perhaps she would grow to love the man she eventually married. Was she really making too much of romantic dreams of a love that she could die for, of a knight in shining armour?

When Teddy left she thought about Simmy and realised that there was a more logical explanation for the changes she had observed in the maid, and innocently presumed were due to the anxieties of nursing. This voyage had forced her to admit that love happened at all ages, and to the most unlikely people. There were many loving couples promenading the deck, completely absorbed in each other, who were neither young nor beautiful, but blissfully happy nevertheless. And every evening, dancing cheek-to-cheek, were couples who had spent half-a-lifetime together. Besides Simson wasn't ugly, she was pleasant-looking, strong and sturdy—a wholesome woman in every way. Of the engineer Bain, Faye had glimpsed only a huddled figure in a sick bay bed.

Perhaps Teddy was wrong, he was prone to exaggeration, she thought as she asked Simson, busily packing: 'How do you feel without all those patients depending on you?'

Simson smiled. 'Fine, Miss. I'm right happy to be back with you again. I feel I neglected you so.'

'Nothing of the kind. I managed perfectly.'

'You fell downstairs—you wouldn't have done that if I had been with you.'

'Or if I had been sensible and worn my spectacles. Anyway, there was no damage.' A pause. 'How would you like to return to nursing again, Simmy, when I get married?'

Simson straightened up from folding a dress. 'Married?' She beamed. 'Oh, Miss, I'm so glad.'

'Not immediately,' Faye said quickly. 'But there is a very strong chance that I will marry. There seems little point in staying at Wainwrights all alone—now—'

'I'll be coming back with you, Miss Faye dear.' The words were loyal but the maid's lips had tightened perceptibly.

'Only if you want to, Simmy.' At the quick frown, Faye added, 'You see, I decided, when I saw how fulfilled you were nursing again, that you still had a vocation. I'd like you to go back to that life again—if it's also your secret wish.'

'You mean, Miss, that you don't want me to come back with you.' Simson's face was a study. Was that gleam of excitement only in Faye's imagination?

'Of course I don't want to lose you, but I no longer feel

that I can selfishly hold you with me, away from a life of your own.'

Simson looked towards the portholes, her folding of clothes mechanical now. 'It's very good of you, Miss, to make this offer, and I do appreciate it. But I don't think I want to go back to nursing again.' Faye's relief was short-lived as the maid continued: 'However, Miss, there is something I ought to tell you. But I don't know quite where to begin.'

Good heavens, the dear soul was actually blushing.

'Mr Teddy may have mentioned it. He has seen me—us—I mean, I have been keeping company with Mr Bain, from the *Odessa*. He's a Scot, same as me, from the same kind of life as I left. In a funny way, he reminds me of the lad I loved and lost long since. Mr Bain went to Russia on a cargo ship twenty years ago and he met and married a girl over there. She died three years ago. There were no bairns to the marriage, so he decided to emigrate to New York and signed on the *Odessa*. You know the rest of the story—'

'I don't really,' said Faye gently.

'Well, at first I thought he was just grateful for me nursing him, especially when he asked me to marry him that first day he was fully conscious again.' Simson glowed with pleasure at the memory. 'I thought he was just being daft—in a fever, like as not. But he wasna'—' She shook her head in wonderment.

'And do you love him too, Simmy?'

'Oh yes, Miss. I know it sounds silly, me being an old maid all these years—and no' a bonny woman, not even when I was a lass did I have a face on me to turn heads. But, Miss, you'll scarcely credit this, when I'm with him, I feel like a blithe and pretty wee thing—sixteen and never been kissed.' She laughed. 'Aye, Miss, I love him, dearly. It was the same for me as it was for him. The first sight of his face, when I cleaned all the oil and tended the scorchmarks—I knew then that I wanted this gentle quiet-seeming man for my own. I want to marry him more than anything else on God's earth, Miss.'

Faye took her hands and they were both silent, then Simmy sighed and, in a practical tone, said: 'Of course,

Miss, I've told him no. That I cannot leave you, not to go back to that great empty house at Wainwrights on your own—'

'Simmy!' Faye leaped to her feet. 'I forbid—yes, forbid you to talk such nonsense.' She seized Simson by the arm and propelled her towards the door. 'Go, at once, and tell him *Yes,* you will marry him—don't protest, do as I tell you. You will marry your Mr Bain because your mistress is also getting married and won't be needing your services any longer—'

At the door Simson paused. 'You're sure, Miss, certain sure, this is what you want?'

'I am—certain sure. Now go!'

Soon afterwards Simmy returned and embraced her young mistress. 'Mr Bain has agreed that I should go back to Wainwrights with you—until after your wedding. He says he doesna' mind waiting another few months when he's been waiting to meet me for years, it seems. And especially as he'll need to look round for a shipyard job. His leg's healing fine—another week or two and he'll be able to discard the crutches.'

Faye smiled. Apparently the quiet Bain had a splendid turn of romantic sentiments which he could express when occasion demanded.

'He's to stay in New York until he can sign on a ship going back to England, or better still, Glasgow. His heart is fair set on seeing Scotland again—'

'And so you'll live there.'

'I hope so, Miss. I think I'm about ready to go home too.'

The last day at sea was one of excitement and jubilation, as well as of leave-takings which no one would regret since this voyage had been uncomfortable as well as longer than scheduled. There was a feeling of parting in the air; in every corridor stewards were busy with trunks and last minute requests from passengers, whilst those who were better organised prepared themselves for the Grand Ball that evening.

For once Faye was immune to the sounds of music and laughter. Her heart felt like lead within her, she felt as if she would never laugh or be merry or light-hearted again—as if all such happiness in life was denied her.

Just before Simson went off-duty to spend the evening with Bain, Teddy appeared at the door. He had been drinking and announced that he was lonely, he would rather be with Faye than partnerless on this special occasion.

He seemed disappointed to see Simson in the background when Faye invited him in.

'I'm sorry, Teddy, could you not partner Miss Schroeder, seeing that she is also alone?'

'Alone! You were never further from the truth there, m'dear. Miss Schroeder—alone! Not as long as your Captain MacManus is on the horizon, I assure you. They have danced every dance together, they are both oblivious of the world, lost in a dream together,' said Teddy bitterly. 'None of the rest of us exists, I can tell you.' He was rather annoyed by this turn of events, since he had hoped to further his cause with Dulcie and take her up on the offer that he suspected had been made outside her cabin door the previous night. 'I will say one thing, they dance divinely together.'

Faye fought back tears at the image conjured up by Teddy's words. She had thought the Captain's divine dancing had been a language spoken for her alone. She had surrounded Captain MacManus with a web of fantasies and day-dreams about his noble character, integrity and courage—and all were wrong, hopelessly wrong. She had been the victim of her own senses and secret desires, her own hunger as a woman. Captain MacManus was a man after all, and Dulcie Schroeder was a very lovely, very warm and desirable woman, with an easy friendly manner with men, which told of considerable experience in the ways of life and love.

'Well, Simmy, is no one going to offer me a drink?' demanded Teddy, staggering towards the sofa.

Imperceptibly Faye shook her head, indicated to Simson: 'Get rid of him.' Wondering, Simson nodded.

'Come along, Mr Teddy, we haven't any drinks here, besides, Miss Faye is very tired. And she has an awful headache—she still has to take care after that fall the other night. Doctor's orders, Mr Teddy,' she added firmly.

Alone and sleepless, the sounds of merriment seeped through the closed door, and Faye turned her face into her pillow and sobbed as if her heart would break. Crying for the Gaffer whose love she had lost and for Gavin MacManus whose love could never be hers.

After tomorrow she would never see him again—

Faye expected the *Atlanta*'s arrival in New York to be a time of great excitement but, secretly surveying the skyline from the window of her stateroom, even the addition of her spectacles could not breathe magic into the scene. She was very disappointed to find New York so ordinary. She had imagined snow and tall buildings and lights everywhere—like the paperweight she had as a child—shake it, and snowflakes drifted romantically, swirling against the sky.

Alas, the prospect before her was like that of any other quayside at the moment of arrival, a grey bustling crowd on a grey blustery day. She sighed, perhaps the greyness emanated from her own sad and leaden heart.

As for Captain MacManus, she saw him once more before she left the *Atlanta*. Deliberately putting off the painful encounter as long as possible, she stayed in her cabin until her luggage was carried away. Then Teddy arrived to tell her that Dulcie was on deck and that Warren Schroeder's automobile was awaiting them both.

As she walked along the promenade deck for the last time with Teddy, she saw, under the awning by the gangway, Dulcie and Captain MacManus deep in conversation.

'I can tell you,' whispered Teddy, 'that's not the last those two will be seeing of each other. I'll bet that's an assignation being made. Well, good luck to them. Your precious Captain seems to be very smitten with Dulcie. And she encouraged him by flirting outrageously at the Ball last night. Not, of course, that Dulcie would want any permanent relationship with a man of that class,' he added with spiteful relish, 'so much below her in every way—'

Faye looked up and saw the Captain approaching. Even his walk, that supple long-legged grace which suggested the athlete rather than the seaman, affected her deeply. She felt her knees trembling and her heart beating far faster than necessary as he bowed over her hand.

'Miss Wainwright—'

But she did not hear his condolences, trying instead to remember everything about him; the black hair which trailed boyishly over his forehead released from the confines of the uniform cap; his eyes, dark and unfathomable; his fine features, the face of a hunter, of a man who prowls, the high cheekbones and wide mouth. She must try to remember him like this forever, and she thought of the long lonely days ahead when this moment would be all she had left of the *Atlanta*.

'Thank you, Captain.'

Her voice was astonishingly emotionless as he released her hand. Had she imagined those scenes of passion? she thought, searching his face for some sign that he too remembered, and seeing nothing but politeness and even a certain relief mirrored in his eyes. He was glad this voyage was over and the leave-taking with her cost nothing, not even regret.

With a great sigh Dulcie bore down upon them and again shook hands with the Captain, smiling deep into his eyes, fluttering long eyelashes at him.

Faye left them and walked with Teddy to the Schroeders' automobile waiting by the gangway. For the ordinary passengers there was still the formality of going through the Customs shed with their luggage. She observed the crowded scene, grateful that Sir Joshua's death and her elevated position on the passenger list had saved her this final ordeal. In the most civilised fashion she had been interviewed by the Customs officials in her cabin. She could have smuggled the Crown Jewels into America successfully, for all the interest they took in her luggage.

Dulcie had also managed to evade the Customs

shed—a word with one of the officials had been enough. However, Teddy was less fortunate and, Earl's son or no, was headed in that direction.

Teddy was to stay at the Waldorf Astoria—he had take a suite of rooms there—until Faye's plans were settled.

'Dulcie actually invited me to stay at their Fifth Avenue place,' he told Faye. 'However, I thought, in the interests of propriety, as we are not yet officially engaged, I should settle for an hotel.'

Faye thought that very decent of Teddy in the circumstances. Except that it wasn't true. Although Teddy could see considerable advantages in having the very willing Dulcie within daily—and more importantly, nightly—reach, while dallying with Faye during the day in the primmest of manners, he decided that his clandestine meetings with Dulcie, which would inevitably follow such close proximity, might have attendant dangers. If anyone got careless, he would lose Faye for ever—and her fortune with her.

Teddy disappeared after kissing Faye's cheek through the automobile window and bowing gravely to Dulcie. Simson was accompanying the luggage in a second automobile and Faye saw her exchange a tender embrace with Bain. She looked up at the ship, but there was no sign of Captain MacManus, no hand raised in farewell. A moment later, the *Atlanta* was out of sight and the tall buildings of New York lay ahead.

At her side, Dulcie chatted endlessly about Captain MacManus. Obviously she was very taken with him, as Teddy had observed.

'Are you to see him again?' asked Faye, knowing that she was inflicting a self-torture upon herself, as she awaited Dulcie's inevitable reply.

'We shall be in touch regularly, before the ship sails back to Southampton. He really is the most fascinating, interesting man I have ever met.'

Faye tried not to listen. She stared out of the window at the grey buildings and fought back tears. She would never see Gavin MacManus again. Never. He was lost to her before he had ever been truly found. And she cursed the fate that denied her even one night of loving him. At least she might then have felt it was worth marrying Teddy, if she had such a blissful memory to sustain her—

How wicked—how divine too—she thought, ashamed and rejoicing at the images which came leaping into her mind.

CHAPTER
THIRTEEN

THE Schroeders' 'little New York home' was a handsome mansion on Fifth Avenue. In the modern style, with carved panelled entrance hall and ceiling, its obvious opulence was a little too grandiose for Faye's taste. The guest suite was delightful though. On the first floor, the windows overlooked Central Park, its trees clad in the first veil-like dusting of snow.

In his study Warren Schroeder was waiting to welcome her. The sight of Faye Wainwright took his breath away, and afterwards he was prepared to swear, although he was not in the least a romantic man, that he knew exactly what it felt like to be struck by Cupid's dart. This was his first sight of Faye the woman, although Faye the child he knew rather better. There was, however, considerable difference between the two images, the gauche shy schoolgirl and the poised and elegant woman, whose mourning clothes gave her an air of mystery.

She was exquisite, delicate as a piece of Dresden china. And Warren knew in that moment that he wished to possess her, to make her his wife. Here was the perfect partner, with beauty, breeding. He found himself suddenly speechless—this man who had everything could hardly believe the extent of his good fortune. To have Wainwrights the house and estate, the Wainwright Line with the legendary *Atlanta*—and now the prospect of this lovely girl to share his life and love.

Faye greeted shyly the middle-aged, balding man who she remembered as Grandfather's friend, who had made occasional visits to Wainwrights and had always brought her some expensive but inappropriate present.

'I am so sorry, my dear. I loved your grandfather dearly.'

There was a new bond between them now, having both lost the man dear to them, and Faye tried to blank from her mind the funeral that was taking place on the other side of the Atlantic.

'It is as he wished,' said Warren Schroeder. 'His last words to me were that you should be spared the harrowing grief of such an occasion.' Faye listened intently as Warren related in detail the scene which had taken place between the two men during their last meeting at Wainwrights. It was almost as if she had been present, she could feel the cool leather upholstery, smell the autumn in the parkland outside the window.

Warren left out one detail only. The financial proceedings which had made him the new owner. Such details must wait until Faye was more composed and ready to receive this vital news. Once she was relaxed and felt comfortably at home . . .

'So Grandfather knew all the time.'

'I guess so, my dear.'

'In that case—' Faye shrugged. She would no longer oppose her Grandfather's last wishes by fighting against what he had planned. Gratefully she returned to her rooms where Simson was unpacking. She stared down at the skeletal branches of the trees in Central Park, a bleak black and white world unrelieved by colour of any kind, desolate as her own heart.

Dulcie had arranged for her New York dressmaker to call with patterns and designs for mourning apparel for Faye to consider. But Faye had little heart for heavy, dark gowns, jet-embroidered jackets and veiled bonnets. Dispiritedly, she allowed Dulcie to choose what was suitable. Life until the next summer was to be a sombre affair for her. She—and Grandfather—had loved bright colours.

Shortly after Faye's arrival, Teddy left his card.

'Who is this man?' demanded Warren of Dulcie, as he read: 'The Hon Edward Haversham,' which had been scored through and 'Your devoted Teddy' substituted.

'He is the son of the Earl of Darleigh. We met on the *Atlanta*.'

'*That* notorious young man we are always reading about in the newspapers?'

'The same.'

'Really.' Warren regarded his sister, smiling. 'Am I to congratulate you, my dear—we could do with an earl in the family. "Your devoted Teddy",' he read again. 'Sounds as if he might be on the hook?'

Dulcie laughed. 'Unfortunately, he isn't *my* devoted anything. You are about to meet the future husband of Faye Wainwright, no less.'

'What did you say?' demanded her brother angrily.

'You heard me, Warren. Faye's intended. And don't you think that is the perfect solution?'

'I do *not*. And without even setting eyes upon him, I guess he would be more suited to you, my dear Dulcie, if you have any sense. Besides I have other plans for that innocent child.'

Dulcie looked up slowly. 'Do you indeed? And may I know what those plans are?'

'You may. Since I already own Wainwrights lock, stock and barrel, I also have hopes, now that I have met the young lady, of making her my wife—the second Mrs Warren Schroeder.'

'She is so very young, Warren.' Dulcie did not want to insult him by adding that they were an ill-matched couple in every way.

'Well, what is wrong with that?' And as though interpreting her thoughts Warren added: 'I know I am forty-five, Dulcie, but may I also remind you that to many women, my age is considered a man's prime.'

Seeing his hurt expression, Dulcie kissed his cheek. 'Then I wish you luck, dearest Warren. All the luck in the world.' And about to leave the study, she decided that he was going to need it. At the door she turned: 'When are you going to tell her that you now own Wainwrights?'

'I shall choose some suitable moment.'

'It is going to be a great shock to her, you know that. To lose her grandfather and then to find in the next breath that with him has gone all her inheritance. The girl is penniless—it won't be easy for her, whatever words you choose. She's proud too.'

'I am sure I can handle the situation, Dulcie.'

'I hope so.' Again she paused. 'Warren—did you really mean what you said, about Teddy being a more suitable husband for me than for her?'

'Of course. He is a fraction too young and as you don't like children, it will be difficult if he has to marry for an heir. And from all I have read in the newspapers, he is also a fraction too wild for domesticity. But the latter will not worry you unduly. Marriage tames most men and—'

'And?'

'And you are a little too old for him, my dear Dulcie. But there are two important levellers. You have money and from all accounts—whispers from London financiers do reach New York from time to time—he needs money badly and so does Darleigh. Besides he is the son of an earl.'

'And I would greatly enjoy the prestige of belonging to one of England's oldest noblest families. And so would you, brother dear, even by marriage.'

Warren bowed. 'We understand each other perfectly.' He regarded her fondly. 'One more thing, Dulcie, before you go. I wish you good luck—'

'Thank you, Warren dear, but I don't think good luck will have much to do with it. Let us say, I will be as ruthless in my pursuit of Teddy Haversham as you will be in wooing Faye Wainwright—'

'What an odd way to put it, sister dear.'

'Besides, I rather think that when Teddy learns that Faye is penniless—and I am not—he will become desperately eager to change his matrimonial plans—with excellent results for both of us.' They beamed at each other delightedly. 'Once Faye realises she is a pauper and that Teddy only wanted her for her money, and that the only way she can hope to continue a life of luxury unimpaired is by marriage with her grandfather's oldest—I beg pardon, dearest—friend, I think there will be great cause for rejoicing all round.'

*   *   *

Warren's opportunity came, with a little connivance between himself and his sister, early that evening. Faye's black velvet gown, as she descended the staircase, owed more to *haute couture* than mourning. Full skirted, its wide embroidered sleeves glittered with jet beads sewn by an army of seamstresses throughout the night. And she would never know how few cents per hour they had earned or of the milliners even now sewing by gaslight in the backstreets of New York in order that a vast sum could be handed over to the designer by Dulcie Schroeder.

Teddy had been invited for dinner. However, he found Dulcie with tickets for the theatre and tales of a sick friend who was unable to accompany her after all. Pouting prettily, she said she had been looking forward to this particular play for some time.

'Warren cannot accompany me with Faye to entertain—his duty as a host—oh, it is all very annoying,' she said preparing to tear the tickets across.

'Wait.' Teddy looked across the drawing-room, where Warren Schroeder in evening dress was an unprepossessing sight—stout, middle-aged, unattractive and certainly old enough to be Faye's father. He decided that Faye could not be left in safer hands for the evening and came to a quick decision.

'May I be allowed the privilege of escorting you, Dulcie—if neither Faye nor your brother object, that is?'

Faye was insistent that Teddy and Dulcie should go to the theatre. All heads turned to Warren. No, he had no objection either, which was not surprising since the little plot had been concocted between Dulcie and himself.

'We might have a little supper afterwards,' said Dulcie as the automobile transported them along Fifth Avenue. She knew of a very elegant 'house' where supper could be had in private rooms. The supper was guaranteed to be excellent. There was also a rather wicked and daring show of nude statues who came to life. 'Companions', were available for unaccompanied gentlemen, but no questions were asked and discreet rooms were provided for assignations requiring privacy. Dulcie felt assured that such an evening would not only be to her own taste and to Teddy's but that their absence would be of great assistance to Warren at the beginning of his courtship of Faye.

After dressing her mistress for dinner, Simson had been allowed the rest of the evening off to see the sights of New York with Bain. If Faye had any qualms about being left alone with Warren Schroeder, these were soon lulled as they were waited upon by an army of servants. At last, Warren suggested they take their coffee in the relaxed atmosphere of the drawing-room. As the door closed on the servants, Faye declined the liqueur which Warren offered. She was already feeling the effects of the excellent wine. There was a splendid fire roaring up the chimney and the room was very comfortable, softly lit—so downy the sofa, she longed to rest her head against the satin cushions, close her eyes and go to sleep!

Suddenly, looking at the strange man sitting opposite her, she knew she was desperately homesick for Wain-wrights. When Warren spoke to her again of going to Virginia in the near future, she shook her head.

'I'm sorry, sir, but I cannot accompany you. I want to return to England, to my own home, as soon as possible—'

'I thought we had agreed that this was what your Grandfather wished—'

'No, sir. I still wish to return to Wainwrights. There are many things I must do there. Surely you can appreciate my desire.' She saw him frown. 'I don't wish to offend you,' she added hastily, 'for I am most grateful for your hospitality—and to Dulcie—your kindness has been greatly appreciated at my time of personal loss and sadness, sir—'

'Please, Faye, do not call me "sir". My name is Warren—and I wish you to use it.'

She smiled. 'I have always called you sir.'

Warren wriggled uncomfortably. 'That belongs to the past—when you were a little girl.'

Faye hung her head and said nothing, and he continued: 'Everything is very different now, my dear. You are a grown-up young lady and that puts an end to any age difference—out of mere respect, of course—between us.'

Faye smiled. 'I understand, Warren,' she added shyly.

There was a moment's silence before he put down his coffee cup and, unlocking a drawer in the secretaire, returned to place a lengthy document before her. The print was small and very close.

'It looks very legal.'

'Shall I tell you what it contains?' When she nodded assent, he said: 'This document transfers ownership of the Wainwright Line and the *Atlanta* to me.' Ignoring her gasp of disbelief, he went on: 'This, my dear Faye, was the final business transacted between Sir Joshua and myself at our last meeting at Wainwrights.'

'I had no idea that he intended selling the Line or the *Atlanta*.' Now that the first shock was over she realised that such an arrangment was the logical one between old friends, especially as Sir Joshua had no heir.

'Your grandfather also managed to conceal from everyone—myself included—that the company was on the verge of bankruptcy.'

'Oh *no*—I can't believe that.'

Warren nodded. 'It is true. He might have survived, but those new engines for the *Atlanta*—'

Faye was no longer listening. Bankruptcy. A word to be avoided, a scandal in the newspapers, shareholders ruined.

Warren had stopped speaking.

'Oh poor dear Grandfather! I never had the slightest idea.' She looked across at Warren. 'Now I have further reason to be grateful to you. To lose his beloved *Atlanta* and maybe bring ruin to many who trusted in him. At least I still have Wainwrights. Perhaps you will help me find a good buyer—a transaction which will leave me with a little money of my own—'

Warren shook his head. 'I am sorry, my dear, to have to break this further piece of bad news. But I am the new owner of Wainwrights—he included the house and estate as part of our business deal. It has to be sold, lock, stock and barrel, to meet the creditors.'

Faye tried hard not to cry. Losing the house was far harder to take than losing the Wainwright Line or the *Atlanta*. For her it was a whole lifetime of memories, the only home she had ever known. She stared at him, white-faced. 'I can't believe it, my home gone. Where shall I go?'

Warren came over, put an arm around her shoulders. 'Please don't distress yourself. Of course you have a home—'

What was he talking about—with Wainwrights no longer hers? He sat down and took her hands. 'Faye, my dearest girl. I realise this is an inappropriate moment. But as you know I'm a business man and I've made my fortune by taking opportunities as they came my way.' He cleared his throat delicately. 'I want you to understand that I hold you in the highest esteem. Even as a child and now as a woman, you were, and are, very dear to me.'

Bewildered Faye stared at him and he continued hastily: 'I would deem it an honour if you would consent to be my wife.'

'Your—wife?' she whispered.

'Yes, indeed. My wife,' he said firmly, trying not to notice her horrified expression. 'I know I must seem rather old for you, but I do have your interests at heart. Marry me and you will not only retain Wainwrights as your home in England, but I am prepared to settle upon you a private income. You will be one of the richest women in the whole of the United States—'

'No!' she interrupted, holding up her hands as if to thrust the image away. 'It is quite impossible, I cannot—'

'Hear me out,' he said sternly. 'Remember, before you say no, that your grandfather would have been the happiest of men had he thought you might take his oldest friend as your husband—'

'Impossible,' she repeated. 'Oh please don't mistake me, sir—I mean, Warren. I am flattered, honoured— any woman would be. You have been so kind, but I could never, never, see you in any other light than as my guardian—my very kind guardian and old family friend.'

Warren was not put out in the least. He could bide his time. He smiled. 'I know it is a little sudden, especially when your emotions are in such turmoil—too many things have happened much too fast. Please don't worry about it, my dear. I am sure that once we get to know each other.' He tried to ignore how she shivered away from his touch on her bare wrist. 'One more personal question,' he added heavily. 'May I ask if you are—er, rejecting me, because of some previous attachment.' She stared at him blankly. 'Is there someone else, Faye?' he demanded sharply, and when she shook her head, he said: 'Not even Teddy Haversham?'

She smiled. 'Teddy has done me the honour to propose and I have promised him that I will consider it. I am afraid I can give you no such hope, sir. I am grateful to you, my grandfather thought highly of you, but I could never, never consider you with any emotion other than respect—and gratitude.'

Warren nodded. 'You may change your mind. In the meantime you are welcome to return to Wainwrights until a buyer is found. Consider it still your home, and while you are there, think also how happy our marriage would have made Sir Joshua.'

Faye looked at him in amazement. How extraordinary that both Teddy and Warren had assured her that by marrying either of them, she would please her grandfather! Surely they did not think that was the important reason for her choice—that she should marry out of a sense of duty to an old man who had loved her devotedly, but had not understood her heart in the least. His standards belonged to an age when such matters were decided by parents rather than their children. She was a modern woman. She would make her own decisions.

'Thank you, sir. Would you please arrange for me to return to England as soon as a passage can be booked on a suitable ship.'

'If you are sure you do not wish to accompany us back to Virginia?' Ignoring her shiver of distaste, he added: 'Very well. Unfortunately the *Atlanta* is under sailing orders for tomorrow—'

Faye sighed with relief. Not the *Atlanta*, that would have been her final inescapable misery.

'She sails with a new captain,' he continued. 'I was very disappointed in MacManus's failure to break the speed-record. He could have accomplished it easily with those new engines. I am afraid I cannot afford such incompetence.'

'Incompetence! Oh how unfair of you to say such a thing! Surely the circumstances are known to you—that he threw away that great opportunity so that he might save human lives. We sailed back for other survivors from the *Odessa,* and we found them,' she added proudly. 'There were passengers mean enough to say Captain MacManus made the wrong decision, that he was wasting time, for no one believed the second boat had not gone down. But he steamed around all night—and found it.'

Slightly mollified, Warren said: 'Well, perhaps his action—without authority—was commendable. Foolish, of course, but commendable on the grounds of humanity. But it is I who own the *Atlanta* now—'

'My grandfather would have behaved exactly as Captain MacManus did, when he was in command.'

'Ah yes, my dear, and look at the miserable state of *his* fortunes! Such philanthropy, I dare say, paved the way for his bankruptcy and the loss of the Wainwright Line.' He paused to allow the information to sink in. 'I build my empire on hard truths, not sentimentality.'

Faye made her escape as soon as she could. In her bedroom she stared out of the window. Where was Captain MacManus now? Somewhere under the same heavy grey skies of New York, she imagined him sitting in a lonely room, watching the snowflakes fall as she did now. Gavin MacManus—without a future, stripped of his command.

She clenched her fists together. It was so unfair. If only she could tell him that he had one friend who believed in him. She knew the Captain well enough to guess that being dismissed for incompetence was the bitterest humiliation his fierce pride could ever suffer.

*　　*　　*

'Did you see this news item?' asked Dulcie at breakfast next morning, brandishing a copy of the *New York Times*. 'Listen to this, Warren. "Following the unexpected death of Sir Joshua Wainwright, owner of the SS *Atlanta*, the famous liner sails back to Southampton later this week, as scheduled. She sails, however, without Captain Gavin MacManus, whose mercy trip to rescue survivors from the Russian emigrant ship *Odessa* cost him the speed-record—and his own command.'

'Give me that,' demanded Warren. Furiously he read the detailed description of an interview with the gallant Captain who told of the events which had led the *Atlanta* to change course after confronting the iceberg, the dramatic rescue, his hunch that there might be others still alive—

'This is intolerable,' shouted Warren, flinging down the newspaper. The slant of the report was silently accusing. It hinted that the new owner, millionaire Warren Schroeder, had heartlessly dismissed the Captain of the *Atlanta*.

'Damnation!'

'Precisely, Warren dear,' said Dulcie. 'It does not add greatly to the benign image you have been at such pains to cultivate,' She looked thoughtful. 'I have one suggestion, which you may care to act upon before any more damage is done—'

'Out with it, then!'

'Well, you would never miss a few thousand dollars, would you? So why not give the gallant Captain the bonus that Sir Joshua promised him? It will all look splendidly philanthropic, especially in the hands of the press: "Even though he failed to achieve the coveted speed-record, the *Atlanta*'s new owner abided by his late friend's wishes, etc. etc. He decided that the Captain should be rewarded for his prompt and courageous action, etc. etc".'

Warren smiled. 'Excellent, excellent! My dear Dulcie, I think you're in the wrong business.' He frowned. 'But where in damnation do I get hold of MacManus.'

Dulcie helped herself to another cup of coffee. 'I dare say that reporter on the *Times* will know his address.'

Watching her brother hurry to the telephone, Dulcie was pleased that Captain MacManus would benefit from her suggestion. She had liked the Captain who had promised much, much more than Teddy Haversham, even as a dancing partner. Their dalliance after the theatre at the discreet little supper-house had been less than perfect, but she was still determined to have the Earl's son. She realised she must be patient and not condemn him too soon. True, Teddy was only a younger son but her spirits had revived considerably when she learned that his elder brother, the heir, was in poor health.

With good fortune he might yet succeed to the title. She could wait and endure a disappointing husband with such a future ahead. Lovers would be easy and plentiful game, once one was the Countess of Darleigh—still beautiful—and rich too.

Captain MacManus had been shocked but not in the least surprised to receive his dismissal from the Wainwright Line. When he learned that the American millionaire Warren Schroeder was the new owner, he realised that this treatment was in accordance with what he would expect from such a man, ruthless in all his dealings.

At his West Street lodgings he was a little surprised, therefore, to receive a messenger bearing a note from Schroeder, requesting him to present himself at the Fifth Avenue address.

He realised as he walked across Central Park that Faye Wainwright was probably staying under the Schroeder roof, awaiting a passage back to England where she was to marry Teddy Haversham, once she was out of mourning.

This piece of news had come from Faye's maid via Peter Bain who he had met also hunting for a new ship. They had spent a pleasant afternoon in a dockside tavern, talking about Scotland, and over a few drams, considerable nostalgia for their native country had been awakened in both men.

The snow was falling heavily by the time he reached

the Schroeder mansion in time to see a familiar figure descend from a carriage.

Teddy Haversham ran up the steps in a manner that clearly indicated familiarity with the house and its inhabitants. Not wishing to encounter him, the Captain lingered on the other side of the road, until the front door opened and Haversham was admitted.

Only then did he ascend the steps and ring the bell. A few moments later he was invited into a large and imposing hall. Its panelling was overshadowed by a sweeping staircase of enormous proportions and it was from there that the Captain felt eyes were watching him very keenly.

Staring up at the half-landing, he glimpsed a slim black-clad figure. Her back was to the stained glass window, her face in shadow, but his sharp eyes told him that it was Faye Wainwright.

But even as he raised a hand in greeting she disappeared rapidly upstairs again. He felt saddened that she still wished to avoid him and that they had parted on such bad terms.

He was ushered into Warren Schroeder's study. The interview with the man behind the desk was brief. Stiffly he handed him a package which he said contained the equivalent of one thousand pounds in dollars.

'For your gallant action, Captain MacManus, which we are pleased to recognise on the grounds of humanity.' He cut short the Captain's thanks. 'That will be all.' As he was leaving Schroeder said: 'One moment. This package arrived for you, delivered here this morning, in the absence of any other forwarding address.'

Thrusting both packages into his pocket, the Captain bowed and left the study a very bewildered man. Although he had lost his command, with this money he could still fulfil that private dream of owning his own ship some day—a very small ship.

Walking across the hall behind the servant who opened the door, he paused and glanced upwards to the landing. It was empty. He sighed deeply, wishing he could have seen Faye once more to wish her well. She was so often in his thoughts, even though he was con-

vinced that they would never meet again. He could
certainly never forget her, or those moments he had held
her in his arms—

Laughter—a mockery to such thoughts—laughter
that was recognisably Haversham's, drifted from one of
the rooms. Captain MacManus delayed no longer, glad
to escape from this onslaught upon his emotions and
thanking good fortune that he had been spared an
embarrassing encounter with Miss Faye Wainwright and
her betrothed.

Descending the steps, he remembered the other package. He recognised the postmark, his mother's familiar
writing. The contents could wait. He was almost afraid
to open it, for its probable contents filled him with
dread.

On the pavement, he paused, glanced towards the
windows upstairs. A curtain fluttered briefly. Could it
be—? He shook his head, and turned his footsteps in the
direction of the Park. He told himself as he hurried along
that the figure he had glimpsed on the stairs could not
have been Faye and that he must cease making her the
object of his fantasies.

Captain MacManus was wrong. The shadowy figure had
indeed been Faye on her way down to join Teddy and
Dulcie in the drawing-room. Every instinct told her that
the uniformed figure dimly-seen in the hall below was
Gavin MacManus.

She longed to rush down and greet him, but the
thought of being coldly and politely received, or hearing
him express conventional sentiments about her health
made her pause. She was little in control of her emotions
where the Captain was concerned. Suppose she broke
down and wept, made an utter fool of herself—

Perhaps he had not seen her. She rushed back to her
room and leaned against the door. Oh dear God, how
much she loved this man, how she longed for him—

Suddenly excitement ran through her veins like wild-
fire. She had a plan. She would wait, go downstairs
casually, and meet him as if by accident as he left
Warren's study. Presumably the visit was connected

with his late command of the *Atlanta* and would take a little time.

They would meet in the hall. She would greet him, warm but friendly, invite him into the drawing-room for refreshment. No—no, that wouldn't do at all—

She wanted to be alone with him. She must think of something else—oh dear, if only she wasn't so confused. Heart thumping, she stared into the mirror, patting her hair to rights, biting her lips to increase their redness. She heard the sound of the front door closing and staring out of the window, watched a blurred figure emerge and hurry down the steps. He paused, glanced towards the window—

It was Gavin MacManus—and he was leaving—leaving without seeing her.

She banged on the glass, called his name. He did not hear. She could no longer see him, he had walked out of her range of vision—and out of her life—for ever.

Without pausing to think, she seized a shawl that lay over a chair, throwing it across her shoulders as she raced downstairs. She completely forgot that it was snowing, that she should take a cloak—a shawl was quite inadequate for that thin black dress. But not caring, she opened the front door, rushed down the steps and into the street.

Was that him now, on the other side of the road, hurrying towards the park gates? If only she had on her spectacles, although she realised they would be little help, for she was almost blinded by the driving snow.

She must reach him, tell him, before it was too late. Tell him—what? That she loved him more than anything in the world, more than life itself. In the face of such a revelation, what did pride matter any more?

Her feet in their thin slippers could feel the chill of the fresh snow. Was that him, just ahead of her, head down against the blizzard?

'Captain—Captain MacManus—'

But he did not stop. She reached his side, seized his arm—and horrified, stared into the face of a complete stranger. Murmuring apologies she stumbled away. The man began to follow her, smiling, mistaking her intentions. But even without her spectacles, there was no mistaking what was in the man's mind. A shawled woman, young and pretty, in an almost empty park, touching his arm.

Out of breath, she stopped at last and, sobbing, realised she had evaded her pursuer. She looked around desperately, unable to bear the thought of returning to the house, half-frozen as she was. As long as she stayed out here in the park, there was a faint hope that the Captain might find her.

Oblivious of ruined slippers, the skirts of her drenched gown clinging icily to her legs and slowing her progress, she stumbled on.

How long she wandered she had no idea, nor how many solitary men she gazed upon, hoping that one would turn and she find herself staring into that beloved face.

Suddenly she became aware that the sky had darkened and gas lamps glowed like a pink pearl necklace through the still-falling snow. There were railings ahead—a gate.

She was so cold, and the snow was blinding, its full force stinging her face. At that last despairing moment, she saw a tall figure a few yards ahead.

'Captain MacManus—Captain! Wait—oh please wait.'

Out of the gate, she began to run across the road. The sound of the approaching carriage, its driver huddled against the blizzard was muffled by the heavy snowfall.

Too late she heard his cry of warning. Too late, someone screamed and then the darkness closed in upon her.

CHAPTER
FOURTEEN

ONE of the Schroeder servants noticed the front door was wide open and the snow driving in. Recriminations swiftly followed and brought forth denials from other members of staff. All were fully aware of Mr Schroeder's feelings on the subject of warmth—and that open doors not only invited draughts but burglars.

Mr Schroeder's secretary came into the hall to investigate and was told by the junior footman that he had glimpsed a woman racing down the steps as he approached the house. Blinded by snow, he had taken her to be a neighbour's servant, sent to deliver a message by hand.

'She was wearing just a shawl, sir, and a dark dress.'

Simson, who had overheard the commotion about the open door, felt a chill of horror at the description. She hurried upstairs and found Miss Faye's room empty, its door wide open.

'Where is Miss Faye?' she demanded.

Dulcie and Teddy joined the others in the hall. Teddy was anxious to leave. Why hadn't Faye come down when Dulcie's maid announced his arrival ages ago?

'Perhaps she is in the study with my brother,' said Dulcie.

'No, Miss Schroeder,' said the secretary. 'Mr Warren is quite alone.'

Dulcie exchanged a guilty look with Teddy. Had Faye got wind of their liaison and been badly distressed?

She sought Warren who said: 'Haven't seen her since luncheon. I imagined she was with you. Have you tried the conservatory—the library? Good heavens, girl, she must be somewhere in the house.'

But she wasn't. At length the junior footman who had seen the black-clad female rushing out in such distress, decided that now that he had time to consider, it *was* Miss Wainwright, definitely!

'I never thought a *lady* would bolt like that—she looked just like a servant on an errand,' he whispered to the secretary.

'Which way did she go?' demanded Warren.

'I'm not sure, sir, I wasn't taking much notice, the snow and all. I *think* she ran straight ahead—into the Park.'

'What in heaven's name would she be doing, rushing into the Park, without a cloak even, in this weather?'

'Something must have alarmed her.' Warren kept repeating the phrase, trying not to look accusingly at his sister and Teddy. He prayed they were always discreet while under his roof.

'What shall we do, sir?' asked Simson, wringing her hands.

Teddy came forward with an idea. 'Maybe she went to my hotel,' he said lamely. 'I'll head over there.' He thought that solution most unlikely, but he was eager to escape.

Simson looked at him quickly. 'She hasn't gone to the hotel. Before I went along to the laundry room, she told me she was going down to see you—and Miss Dulcie.'

Again Warren looked at the two of them angrily. What had she interrupted, he wondered. Now indecisively they stood in the hall, all waiting for him to say something. Should they wait or set off with a search party? The weather was worsening steadily. The servants, respectfully awaiting orders, exchanged significant glances. Ladies did not rush—improperly clad—out of Fifth Avenue mansions in a snow-storm like this one.

Simson who had disappeared upstairs returned carrying a thick cloak. 'I'll go across and see if I can find her. Maybe she's met with an accident—fallen and hurt herself in the snow.' Simson sounded very practical and the suggestion was seized upon thankfully by everyone. But in spite of her words, she was completely at a loss and very, very frightened by Faye's dramatic disappearance and her inexplicable behaviour.

'Has she ever done anything like this before, Simson?' asked Warren in a whisper.

'Never, sir, to my certain knowledge. But she did have a bad fall on the ship—knocked unconscious for a while.'

'Oh! Do you think she's lost her memory then?'

'I don't know what to think, sir, I honestly don't.' And so saying, Simson set off, hunched against the blizzard.

Ten minutes later, she found her young mistress, lying by the roadside, surrounded by a crowd of passers-by.

'Let me through—let me through!'

'Nobody touched her, lady,' said the cabby. 'I managed to swerve, thank God. She just fell down—slipped on the snow. Lucky she didn't go under the wheels—or the horses' hoofs.'

Simson bent over her, chafing her hands. With a moan, Faye's eyes fluttered open. She tried to sit up.

'Where am I? What happened?'

'You slipped on the snow, Miss Faye.' Simson's hands moved over her expertly. 'Are you in pain? No. Then can you stand, do you think?' She helped her to her feet.

'I'm not hurt, Simmy, I just got a terrible fright. I thought—well, the horses seemed to be right on top of me.'

'Wonder you weren't killed, miss,' said a bystander.

'Shouldn't be running about like that in this weather.'

'Was she killed, Mom?' demanded a shrill voice on the outskirts of the crowd.

Faye stared at the curious faces around her. 'Please get me back, Simmy. Yes, I can walk—'

Simson threw the cloak around her. She was soaked to the skin, her clothes freezing about her legs.

'Jump in, lady,' said the cabby, greatly relieved not to have a corpse on his hands. 'I'll have you home in no time.'

Teddy met them at the door and carried her upstairs. She seemed too stunned to speak, so shaken by the near-accident and so frozen that she felt she could never again be warmed, not even by the hot bath that Simson quickly drew.

*   *   *

Simmy's prompt ministrations, alas, were not sufficient to prevent the severe chill with a high fever that followed. For three weeks Faye lay at the very brink of death, while Simson devotedly nursed her back to a life for which she seemed to have complete indifference. And the maid learned the reason for that extraordinary flight into the snow. For in her delirium, Faye whispered one name, over and over, calling for him, trying to reach him, but Simmy gave no indication that she shared Faye's secret.

When at last she was able to leave her bed and sit weakly by the roaring fire downstairs, one of her first visitors was Teddy. He talked his usual affable nonsense and made her laugh, but there was a grimmer purpose behind his visit. He needed to know that she was strong enough not to have hysterics before he brought up the delicate and painful subject. Guiltily, he asked if she still wished to marry him.

'Still, Teddy?' She smiled wanly. 'I wasn't aware that I had ever said yes.'

Teddy straightened his tie and coughed apologetically. 'Well, old girl, it's like this, you see. I realise how deuced foolish I behaved, that I made a great pest of myself with my attentions and that you never loved me.' He paused, but when she offered no comment, continued hastily, 'I realise there's not much hope that you will change your mind, because we've been friends for a long time now—and if you'd wanted to be more than that, you'd have felt differently ages ago.'

Faye thought the speech sounded oddly rehearsed, as she said: 'Being friends isn't the least like being in love, Teddy. I tried to tell you that.'

'And I was the world's greatest fool not to listen. I do know now—that you were right.'

And in that moment Faye decided she liked him very much indeed, her dear old friend Teddy, amusing and so kind.

'Go on,' she said encouragingly.

'Well, you see, it isn't at all the way Dulcie and I feel about each other. We have had much more time together since you were ill. And—well—she has done me the honour of promising to be my wife.'

Faye clasped her hands together. 'Oh, Teddy, that is marvellous news. I'm delighted for you both—I'm sure you'll be very happy.' As she said the words, Faye realised she was being somewhat over-confident, but she allowed her romantic and charitable feelings to put at rest qualms about such a marriage.

A week later, Warren and Dulcie decided to visit relatives in Boston. Not unnaturally, they wanted Teddy to accompany them. Faye was to make herself at home while they were gone, consider the house and servants hers to command.

The snow had vanished and there followed a mild spell of almost spring-like weather. Faye was once again able to take short walks in the park, leaning on Simson's arm. One day, after such a jaunt, she handed the maid a box containing her jewels, and most of her clothes with instructions to sell or pawn them for whatever money she could raise.

'All I require is enough money to buy two sailing tickets on the next ship back to England. Straight away, Simmy—as soon as we can.'

'What about the Schroeders, Miss?'

'They are a dear kind pair, and Warren has told me that I may stay at Wainwrights as long as I like, until a buyer can be found. To put it in his words: Property loses value when it lies empty! But, Simmy, I know now I can never go back there. Besides, I had a letter yesterday from Mary. She and David were at the funeral, you know. And they have invited me to Hawkswell for Christmas, and to stay as long as I like afterwards. And you are to come with me to Yorkshire, Simmy dear, if Bain can spare you.'

'You can rely on that, Miss Faye—for as long as you need me. Besides, Bain will need to stay at the sea until we can get a home together.'

'Oh, Simmy, I'll be so grateful to have you with me for a little while longer. Perhaps we could go to Wain-wrights—just long enough to gather my most precious possessions. I'm sure one visit will be more than enough,' she said sadly.

'Have you no plans for the future, Miss?'

'None. Just the hope that if the worst comes to the worst, I might earn my living as a governess. At least Grandfather saw to it that I was well-educated. Perhaps I could be a companion. I have friends with elderly aunts,' she said cheerfully, 'who still like to travel, but are too infirm to do so alone. Can you imagine me as a prop to the aged, Simmy? Perhaps that is my role in life.'

'I'm sure it won't come to that, Miss. Some nice young gentleman will come along, mark my words—'

Faye looked sad. 'I shouldn't take any bets on that, Simmy dear. I'm not at all sure that I'm cut out for marriage.'

'You've never been short of proposals, Miss,' Simson reminded her. 'Suitors were always appearing at Wainwrights, as I remember.'

'But was it *me*—or my fortune—they wanted? We shall soon see! Now that I am as poor as the proverbial church mouse, the story may be very different—'

'Oh, Miss, don't look on the black side yet.'

'No, Simmy, not even after Mr Teddy?'

Simson was silent, her lips pursed. She had been bitterly disappointed in Mr Teddy. Planning to marry that American divorcée, Dulcie Schroeder! She could hardly believe that the two of them were in love, after the fuss Mr Teddy had made over Miss Faye all this long time. And her by far the nicer of the two ladies. But Simson wryly suspected that the Schroeder fortune was the inducement. Mr Teddy needed money desperately and Miss Faye was now penniless.

Faye was agreeably surprised when Simson returned with the news that she had raised five hundred dollars on the jewels. Faye's delight and glad acceptance did not show the least curiosity as to where this vast sum of money had been obtained.

'Bain has his uses, living on the seamier side of the city, Miss.' And she put two tickets before her. 'He has signed on as engineer on a cargo ship called the *Freedom*. They are sailing for Southampton and have room for a couple of passengers.'

'Oh, Simmy, that is the most wonderful news. Just to

think we'll be back in England soon.'

'We can put our luggage on any time, Miss, seeing the ship's in dry dock, awaiting loading.'

'Let's do it right away,' said Faye, hugging the maid: 'Are you happy now?'

Simson smiled. 'Never been happier in my whole life. If only I could see you settled I would be the most contented woman in the universe—especially now. Miss Faye, Bain and I want to get married before we leave New York. There seems no reason for delaying at our age. Besides, honeymoons are for rich folks,' she said as together they packed Faye's few remaining possessions into one large trunk.

The hired carriage set them down by the *Freedom's* berth. A dull December day, with a piercing wind did not restore Faye's spirits, since nothing could have been further from the grandeur of the *Atlanta* than the sturdy little cargo ship flying the Red Ensign of Britain's Merchant Service.

As Faye walked up the gangway, she could not help remembering her grand entrance on the *Atlanta*—two white Mercedes on the quayside, and the first sight of Captain MacManus's face sternly regarding her somewhat late arrival. And how he had despised her for all that luggage!

She sighed. If she were grateful for anything, it was that since leaving the *Atlanta,* Simson had not once mentioned the Captain's name. He might never have existed. Everyone seemed to have forgotten him, except herself, for he continued to torment her dreams, although she set thoughts of him firmly aside in her waking hours.

The *Freedom* was due to sail at midnight on the following day, just a few hours after Simson's wedding. Matters could not have worked out more conveniently for them all, thought Faye. Her heart was sad, but it was good to be going home again. She decided she had best get used to her new station in life and the first thing was to be able to carry her own valises—she might be called upon to do a lot of this in future. So, firmly clutching one in each hand, she watched her trunk being hoisted aboard. Destined for Hawkswell, it would remain with Mary and David until she had found a situation.

Simson led the way to the passengers' quarters; the steps were steep and dark. 'The cabin is very small,' she warned. 'Just large enough for the owner who sometimes travels with the ship and brings his little family along—especially on short trips to Europe in the summertime. Children like that—oh, do take care, Miss—did you not see—'

'Wait a moment, Simmy.' And with a sigh of resignation. Faye took out her spectacles. If she must learn to carry her valises with sturdy independence, she had better get used to seeing the hazards ahead, since she could no longer have Simson acting as her eyes.

Besides, pretence was foolish indeed, when there was no one left to impress. She had worn her spectacles several times when Simson wasn't present and as always she was both delighted and astonished at the bright world they revealed. How sparkling and crystal clear, as everything came sharply into focus. How lovely to see distant horizons emerging from the blurred vision she had suffered all these years.

Oh dear, how silly she had been to miss so much that was happening just beyond her nose, and all to appease her own vanity.

The owner's cabin was small and unpretentious, but the furniture and the leather chairs were spick and span, the brass fittings gleamed with polish. The sense of pride indicated by the *Freedom's* neat, well-scrubbed decks, continued inside. Here was a ship that was loved.

And there on the wall, a photograph of a middle-aged, uniformed Captain, seated with his wife and children, stared down at her.

'Captain Horatio Jones of the SS *Freedom*,' said the caption. Despite his stern expression, she decided that Captain Jones must have a kind heart, for he was giving Bain and Simmy a cabin of their own, being newly-weds.

She looked at his wife, holding her husband's hand, smiling and confident, four attractive children, the boys handsome in sailor suits, the girls in white dresses.

She closed her eyes. If only—if only she could hope

for such a future, for such happiness, twenty years from now. If only, whispered her heart, she could look once more upon the beloved face of Captain Gavin Mac-Manus!

Aware of a shadow in the doorway behind her, she turned round, but it was only Simmy who had been inspecting, with Bain, their own cabin.

'Ready to leave when you are, Miss.'

On the way back to the Schroeders', they discussed the wedding arrangements. Simmy and Bain would be married in St James' Presbyterian Church with Faye as bridesmaid and a sailor acquaintance of Bain's as best man.

Before she retired that evening, Faye wrote to Warren Schroeder thanking him for his hospitality and telling him of her unexpected change of plans. As she handed over the note, she doubted whether the servants would regret her departure. The housekeeper plainly regarded Miss Wainwright and her maid as usurpers. She had already crossed swords with Simson over minor domestic trifles and Faye felt that when they took their departure, the door would be slammed upon them with considerable alacrity.

She slept little that night. What dreams came were cruelly vivid—of Gavin MacManus. She awoke in tears, feeling that hearts did break, in real life too, not just in fairy-tales!

She had never felt less like going to a wedding. All she longed for on this earth was to burrow deep into the pillows and seek oblivion. Anything—anything but to dress and smile. But she could never spoil her dear unselfish Simmy's happiness. She owed it to her to put on a smile, to seem light-hearted and, if only for a few hours, to try and set aside this leaden weight of grief in her heart.

And then, thankfully, once the *Freedom* sailed at midnight, she could close the cabin door and let fall the mask . . .

As they prepared to leave—both of them for very different reasons unable to face either breakfast or luncheon, much to the cook's displeasure—Faye wished a little of her fortune remained so that she could give Simson a substantial wedding present.

Instead, she pinned on Simson's jacket her most precious possession, the heart-shaped pearl and diamond brooch which her father had given to her mother on their engagement.

Simson's eyes filled with tears. 'Oh Miss, Miss, I can't take that from you.'

'Don't you like it, Simmy? You always said you admired that piece more than any other. That's the only reason why I didn't let it go with the rest—so that you should have it as your wedding present.'

Simson took Faye's hands and kissed them. 'Miss, it's far too grand for the likes of me, that's all. It's for a fine lady like yourself—'

'Like I used to be, Simmy dear,' Faye corrected her. 'But not any more. Now, for the first time, I've got to learn what it would have been like to have been born humble—and you've got to teach me, Simmy. Teach me that, as you have taught me everything else I value. You will be patient with me, won't you? I'll probably make terrible mistakes until I get my bearings.'

As the carriage rolled away from Fifth Avenue, she sighed. 'I wish more than anything else that I could afford to take you both to the Waldorf Astoria for your wedding breakfast—'

'Breakfast at this hour of the day, Miss!'

Faye smiled. 'They always call it such—by tradition. Faye Wainwright, heiress, could have taken you, but alas, not Faye Wainwright, impoverished gentlewoman.'

Simmy took her hand. 'Wedding breakfasts—as you call them—at big hotels are for rich folks, Miss Faye, not for the likes of Bain and me. The Scotch Tavern is more in our line. Bain has lodgings next door. Good plain Scots food they serve, with a fiddler or two and the floor cleared for the dancing.'

'I didn't know you danced, Simmy!'

'As a lass I did,' Simson smiled shyly. 'But the chance never came once I was a respectable nursemaid at Wainwrights. Sir Joshua would never have approved.'

'Tell me about this Scotch Tavern.'

'Well, a lot of the older folks started it. They came here to New York as bairns when their parents were driven to emigrate after the Highland Clearances. They've kept the old traditions alive and still speak the Gaelic—although I gather the new generation scorn that sort of thing and prefer to consider themselves *real* Americans!'

The carriage stopped and Simson looked out of the window.

'There's the church now, Miss Faye.' She leaned back for a moment. 'I can hardly believe it—in a few minutes I'll be Mrs Peter Bain—me, plain Annie Simson, an old maid past forty. Would you pinch me, please, Miss Faye—see if I wake up.'

'I think I'll just kiss you instead—there!' chuckled Faye. Serious again, she said: 'Dear Simmy, I wish you all the happiness in the world, for no one deserves it more than you.'

The Presbyterian Church, Calvinist and candleless, was dark inside. The unseen organist played 'Where sheep may safely graze', as the bride in her best navy blue costume walked down the aisle, accompanied by Faye, in her black gown and cape.

Two shadowy indistinct figures in uniform moved forward. Bain came to Simmy's side and took her hand. Faye watched them exchange a loving confident smile. She found the dimly lit interior of the church oppressive and wished she could put on her spectacles for a closer look at the proceedings.

Beyond the couple, still in shadow, stood Bain's best man. Faye was curious to see him.

He was tall—there was something even in the dimness that struck her as oddly familiar—

Heart hammering, she blinked rapidly, trying desperately to get him into focus. Poor light and an aching, longing heart were playing tricks on her. She was imagining things—

She blinked, looked again.

Was it—?

Could it be—?

Aware of her eyes, the man turned, gravely saluted her.

It was!

'Dearly beloved, we are met together to join in holy matrimony, this man and this woman—'

Clutching Simmy's bunch of flowers, Faye tried in vain to stop her hands shaking. She had to press her knees hard together to stop them trembling, to stop herself falling on to that cold stone floor.

This was awful—awful—her worst nightmare was coming true.

Oh how could Simmy and Bain have played this cruel heartless trick on her. How could they? And then she remembered that Simmy was guiltless. How was she to know of her mistress's feelings for the Captain, which she had been at such pains to conceal? As for Bain, he had probably chosen the Captain since he was available at short notice. And Bain had excellent reasons to thank Captain MacManus for his present happiness—his survival, recovery and his meeting with Annie Simson.

'Wilt thou, Peter Bain, take this woman, Annie Simson—'

'Wilt thou, Annie Simson, take this man, Peter Bain—'

There was a slight pause while Gavin MacManus searched for the wedding ring. And as the two moved forward for the blessing, he took his place unsmiling at Faye's side.

'I now declare you man and wife—whom God hath joined together, let no man put asunder. You may kiss the bride.'

Faye could hold back tears no longer. Tears for her own humiliation mixed with joy for her beloved Simmy whose face had taken on the sudden radiance of a young girl. She looked as if the years had slid away. She was transformed. And Faye realised that happiness was the greatest beautifier in the world. Happiness defied time. How could she have ever imagined this new Simmy as plain? Love created its own miracles.

Love—Faye looked at Gavin MacManus and felt as if she could no longer contain the emotions that overwhelmed her. She was glad as they walked towards the vestry of his steadying hand on her arm. A hand so warm, even comforting. Oh dear God, she longed to cry out. How could she get through the remainder of this day? she thought desperately. He was almost certain to accompany them to the reception—what then? To sit at his side making polite conversation through the passing hours, while inside her heart bled—

Love—love—their footsteps on the stone floor seemed to echo the word. Love—love, the triumphant wedding march proclaimed, as the organist reached a crescendo.

Love was everywhere—

Oh dear God, she prayed. Please let me die—now.

She opened her eyes and the smiling face before her was that of the minister handing her a pen to sign the register. Now they were shaking hands, walking down the aisle, out of the church. Snow was falling gently, like confetti on the newly-weds.

Side by side with Gavin MacManus, she was smiling, kissing Simmy and Bain, waving to them as they stepped into the waiting carriage.

Gavin was laughing. She hardly recognised his care-free happy face as he cheered them on.

At last the carriage rolled out of sight.

At last she could escape. Make her apologies. Go back to the ship. Never see Gavin MacManus again.

CHAPTER
FIFTEEN

THERE was no escape.

'This way, Miss Wainwright.' The Captain was ushering her towards the carriage which had drawn up.

'No.' She stood firm on the pavement, arms clasped to her sides.

The Captain frowned and, ignoring her protest, tried to propel her forward. 'Come along, Miss Wainwright.'

'*No.* I have said no!' She stood her ground firmly.

'What is wrong?' He sounded concerned as he looked into her face. 'Are you ill? You're very pale.'

Please don't sound tender, caring, she thought, closing her eyes. Please stay stern and forbidding. Make it easy for me to leave you, to escape. Never, *never* to see you again!

'I am quite all right,' she said, 'if you will be so good as to put me into a carriage.' How calm her voice, how at variance with the roaring tumult inside her.

The Captain bowed. 'Delighted, Miss Wainwright. That is precisely what I intend to do—to escort you to the Scotch Tavern.'

'I am not going to the Scotch Tavern,'

'But—'

'Do you not understand? I am not going anywhere— not with you, Captain MacManus.'

He looked at her and sighed heavily. 'Then where do you wish to go?' he asked with weary patience.

'I wish to go to the docks. I join a ship to Southampton. We sail tonight.'

'Oh, don't talk such daftness, Miss Wainwright. You can't sit in a ship all day. What's the matter with you?' In anger he was suddenly more Scotch than she remembered from the *Atlanta*. 'Now do stop being a silly wee lassie. Think of someone else for a change—'

That stung her!

'—You're surely not going to desert Mrs Bain at her wedding reception? And you her bridesmaid! What will she think of that? You can't spoil her great day like this—'

It was true. She couldn't go off and leave Simmy without a word of explanation. Even if she sent a message via the Captain that she was feeling ill—knowing Simmy, her maid would insist on leaving the reception and rushing to the *Freedom*. No, for Simmy's sake she had to carry on this intolerable farce for another few hours. Then, please God, she'd be aboard the *Freedom*, able to close her cabin door—and weep—and weep. She felt her unshed tears were endless, an ocean of sorrow.

The Captain handed her into the waiting carriage. She shrank as far away from him as possible, remembering with shame all those dreams of falling into his arms, holding him. Kissing him . . .

She looked at his profile staring into the street. He was a stranger again, he had forgotten her presence. A man unknown. She found herself blushing to remember small intimacies, the time—the time she had been ready to give herself to him aboard the *Atlanta*. Shame crawled over her. Small wonder he was distant, if he too remembered. A wanton hussy—

He was probably embarrassed as she at this unexpected meeting, and cursing Bain, too.

'Here we are. It wasn't far.'

He helped her down and from the tavern streamed the sound of bagpipes. As they emerged from the dusk, shaking off the light snowflakes, Faye had a bewildering out-of-focus glimpse of antlered deer heads peering down at her from the walls, of tartan drapings and vast heather-clad hills above a sparkling loch. For a wild moment she wonder if she had been transported bodily across the Atlantic to be set down at a window in Scotland. And then she realised that some nostalgic artist had been at work and what she beheld was a huge painting covering one wall.

'Come awa' in, lass'

'Ye'll tak a wee dram?'

'*Slainte! Slainte!*' Glasses were raised to toast the newly-weds.

Faye was kissing a radiant Simmy. 'Are you happy, Mrs Bain?'

'Oh yes, so happy,' sighed Simmy, pressing her hand. But her smile faded at the expression on Faye's face, so frail and delicate-looking since that terrible fever had taken the flesh from her bones. Suddenly Simson felt ashamed, yes, ashamed of having so much happiness, when her beloved Miss Faye had so little. Their positions had been reversed with a vengeance. Only a cruel and heartless fate could have twisted their destinies to allow this bleak lonely future for the girl she had served so devotedly all these years.

Bain came to his wife's side, linked arms with her and beamed at Faye, who raised her glass to them.

'Long life and happiness. God bless!' The fiery spirit made her choke, burnt her throat, but she finished it to the last drop.

Now there were dancers on the floor, cleared of its tables. Not the decorous waltzes and quadrilles of *Atlanta* days, but wild skirling reels and jigs, accompanied by the dancers' shrill cries.

Before she could protest, Gavin MacManus was leading her into the fray. He did not seem to notice that she was in mourning, or even remember. Now she was dancing, held close in his arms, her feet following him instinctively in the intricate square dance, her body following him hungrily, in an ecstasy of recognition— betraying her—

On and on, breathless, handed from partner to partner in the reel, then laughing back to Gavin. Now he was holding her close, the music had changed to a dreamy waltz. Now it was as if the musicians played for them alone. Conscious of his warm hand on the small of her back and his shoulder near her forehead, her body, her very soul, refused to obey her commands. As if it tore apart from her mind and recognised with joy and abandon this man she had found again.

She found herself staring up into his face and knew she could never stop loving him.

Never stop, she sobbed, no, not even if this night is all we shall ever have together—

Wild applause greeted the dance's end and it was speedily followed by another reel. There were shouts to Gavin in a strange tongue and he was replying in what she realised must be Gaelic. Now he was raising his glass to the happy pair, being slapped on the back by the bridegroom.

As he led her to a table, he still held her hand tightly. She looked at the strong fingers, brown and shapely, entwined in hers. Suddenly he was regarding her, unsmiling.

'Faye—oh my dear, will you ever forgive me? I was carried away—I had entirely forgotten—' and gently he touched the sleeve of her mourning gown.

His voice trailed off and she shook her head. 'I have to be honest, for one small moment I had forgotten too. I think Grandfather would have wanted it that way. He wouldn't think it disrespectful, for he hated black gowns and mourning. He wanted everyone to be happy when he had gone—you know that.' Faye sighed. 'I'm sure he doesn't feel his memory is being insulted—and if others do, then their opinions matter little to me.'

He was silent, then he asked: 'Would you like to dance again?'

'No, I would rather talk.'

'You still want to talk to me?'

'Of course.'

He regarded her with that slow smile she loved. 'You don't hate me all that much any more, do you?'

'Hate you,' she echoed. 'Oh no, of course not, whatever gave you that idea?'

'You have reason.' His face was sober now. 'I treated you badly, Faye. I owe you an explanation—'

'Please—no.'

'Then why did you avoid meeting me that day I came to the Schroeders'—'

So he didn't know!

'I saw you on the landing, then you disappeared before I could speak to you. Of course, I understood—after all that had happened—you had a perfect right—

after that night on the *Atlanta*—'

He knew by the swift colour which arose in her face, that she too remembered.

'The reason for it—well—'

'No, please, Captain,' she interrupted. 'There is no need to be embarrassed on my account. I'd rather not discuss it—in fact, I had quite forgotten the incident,' she lied.

'Is that why you blush—and why your hands tremble, Miss Wainwright?' His voice was mocking and his sudden return to formality hurt her. 'I think you should hear me first before you condemn me as an out-and-out scoundrel. The story goes back a long way. My mother was the laird's only daughter. She fell in love with my father, a servant on the estate and, alas, he got her with child. Her family promptly disowned her, so she married my father and went with him to one of the outer islands of the Hebrides, where I was born. Father had little to offer this delicate cultured lady and love soon died when she was forced into the gruelling life of a poor crofter-fisherman's wife. She never forgave *her* father and when he died and an elderly cousin—a very remote one from Glasgow—inherited, she fought bitterly to regain what was rightfully hers under Scottish law—whereby a daughter has equal rights. She was doing it for me, she said—but all I wanted was to escape, to go to sea. When my father died, she hardly shed a tear—it was dreadful for a boy to watch, to try to understand her bitterness—'

Faye didn't hear the end of ths story for at that moment the wedding feast was announced and they took their places at the table. The Scottish meal was humble and nourishing, it had fed the poor of Gavin's land for generations. Haggis, potatoes and mashed turnips, Atholl Brose for dessert and all washed down with fiery whisky drams.

Faye was separated from Gavin now, for he sat on the other side of Simmy. She tried to remember his bewildering story but this new revelation about his past did not make him dearer to her. Should he be the Lord of the Isles himself, she still wished for no castle, no land and no title—ever again. She chided herself for such imaginings, as she never expected to see him again after this day. Still it was ironic that her humble but proud Captain MacManus might, but for the accident of birth—have been a Scottish laird in disguise.

All around her there was wild applause. The Captain was making a speech—in Gaelic—she couldn't understand a word. Bain was replying in English—lifting his glass to her. More applause, more drams, and then the celebration was at an end. The tavern was to be transformed for its normal evening customers.

Simson, whose training died hard, came across carrying Faye's cape. 'You come along in the carriage with us, Miss Faye.'

Faye glanced round. She had lost Gavin MacManus in the crowd as the guests converged upon the floor to join hands in 'Auld Lang Syne.' Outside the tavern, she said:

'The Captain—where is he?'

'I don't know, miss.'

Bain emerged from the building and left his group of friends. 'The Captain, Miss. Said he had an appointment.' He smiled. 'Sent his apologies, Miss.'

His *apologies*. Her eyes filled with tears. It was more than she could bear. Not even a goodbye kiss to remember. Oh how could he be so callous!

She shook her head. No, that was unfair. What reason had she ever given him to believe that she loved him?

It was dark when they reached the *Freedom* and a light covering of snow lay underfoot. The cold glittery sky was full of frosty stars and Faye, longing for oblivion, felt her face stiff and aching with the effort of smiling, of talking enthusiastically about the events of the wedding and who at the Scotch Tavern was related—talking of reels—of food—and who had too many drams taken—

If only she could be alone. Would she never be permitted the luxury of weeping in the darkness? She felt suffocated by unshed tears.

Simmy helped her down the steps. 'I'll see you safe to your cabin before I turn in,' said Simmy and when Faye protested that it should be the other way round, that she should prepare the bride to retire, Simmy laughed.

'Old habits die hard, Miss Faye,' she said, turning up the lamp.

Blinking in the sudden brightness, Faye saw lying on the bed a pile of furs which looked familiar.

'Simmy—my coat! How did it get here?' she said, holding the soft warmth against her cheek. 'I thought they went towards the cost of the tickets. Bain didn't sell them? I don't understand—'

'You're to regard them as a present, Miss.'

'But—'

'I'll be back later, Miss.' She put a finger to her lips and listened. 'Bain'll be talking to our captain. He's just come aboard. I dare say he'll want to meet you too, Miss Faye.'

Before Captain Jones appeared, Faye decided she had better inspect her appearance. She put on her spectacles and stared into the tiny mirror. That was better. She unpinned her hair and decided that she looked far from the vision who had sailed for Halifax on the *Atlanta*. None of the passengers would recognise her in the plain black dress, bespectacled.

She was so immersed in her reflection that she hardly heard the door open softly behind her. Instinctively she thrust her spectacles into her pocket and peered into the dim light at the shadowy figure in the dark corridor.

'Captain Jones?'

'May I come in?' The newcomer was Gavin Mac-Manus. 'I see you have discovered your furs. It occurred to me that you'd need those—the voyage will be chilly. I also redeemed—I think that is the phrase—the jewels that Bain had to dispose of to pay for your passage aboard the *Freedom*.' He thrust a small jewel box into her hand. 'Alas, I was too late to save them all, some had been sold.'

Faye opened the box in wonder. 'You are so kind, Captain. I never expected this.' Her eyes filled with tears. 'The jewels mean little to me now, I'm afraid, but they might hopefully provide an insurance for my future. I am afraid I may have to face some grinding poverty, until I find a post—as governess—'

'A governess—that is your plan?'

'Indeed, yes,' she tried to sound pleased and cheerful at the prospect. 'I have little desire to return to London and as I am going to friends in Yorkshire, I dare say there may be opportunities to find a suitable situation.' He said nothing and she continued brightly, 'I'm rather looking forward to my new life.'

The Captain remained silent and suddenly embarrassed, ashamed of her lies, Faye held out her hand. 'I don't know how to thank you for your kindness. And I do appreciate your coming aboard to wish us *bon voyage*.' She smiled. 'I thought I might never see you again.'

He smiled at last. 'We won't be saying goodbye for a week or two yet. And not even then, unless you wish—'

'You mean you are travelling to Southampton with us, Captain?' Faye's heart leaped with sudden joy. 'I hadn't realised that you also had a passage booked—'

'Not a passage, my dear. I sail as captain of the *Freedom*—'

'Oh, I'm so glad—glad for you. And as you will be in England for a while, perhaps we can find some means by which I can repay you for taking my furs—and my jewels—out of pawn. Perhaps there will be a little money left after the sale of Wainwrights—'

Gavin MacManus seized her hands and clasped them firmly to his chest. 'There is only one way you can possibly repay me. Love me, Faye *mo gradh*, as I love you. Stay with me always, give me your love, for without it I am nothing. My dearest girl—don't you know by now that I love you more than anything in the world—more than life itself,' he whispered.

'Oh Gavin, Gavin, I love you, too. So much—I have longed for you—' Suddenly she was weeping and he held her close, kissing her with growing passion—

'Why weep, my dearest? I am here and I am all yours.'

'For a while, maybe, and then we will part again—'

He held her chin cupped in his hand. 'No, my dearest one, for always, if you want me.'

'Always?'

'Yes. The *Freedom* is mine. I bought her with the bounty Schroeder gave me—a down-payment, that is. She is yours to share with me, as my wife.'

'Oh Gavin—my love, my love.'

She was in his arms and there was no need for further words, for they were in a land they had discovered long ago, where words are superfluous for arms and lips that know well the language of love and recognise the fires of desire.

Some time later, Gavin said: 'I had never noticed until I came into the cabin this evening that you wore spectacles.'

'I don't, except in dire necessity, they're hideous—'

'Put them on!' He regarded her, head on one side. 'They are not hideous and you look lovely as ever—even more dignified and beautiful.'

'You can't mean that—'

'I do. And you must wear them, because I am your lord and master and I command you to!' he added laughing. 'Besides I can't afford to have you falling down ship's ladders and breaking your lovely neck.'

Faye looked at him and saw him clearly for the first time. His face so dear and handsome, his magnificent eyes and fine strong mouth. 'You mean you don't mind?'

'My dearest one, do you think that any man who loved you, would love you less for such a reason.' He laughed. 'Only a woman could believe that—men are much too vain! Tell me, how will you like living aboard the *Freedom?*'

'I shall love it. If it means that I can see you nearly every day for the rest of my life.'

'And every night too, don't forget,' he whispered and added casually, 'Unless you'd like to go back to the Hebrides and live in a draughty ruined castle there? My mother's letter is triumphant—victory at last—the lawsuit won!'

She shuddered. 'No more castles, Gavin dearest—I beg of you. And I want only one title: Mrs Gavin MacManus. However, perhaps we could afford a *tiny* cottage somewhere,' she paused and glanced shyly at the picture of Captain Jones and Family: 'A cottage with roses round the door, for when we have babies, so that we can wait there ready to welcome you home from sea.'

Gavin chuckled. 'Sweetheart, you do rush ahead,

don't you!' Pausing to kiss her again, which took a little while, he said at last: 'Come on deck, there is something I want you to do.'

Leading the way, taking her hand up the ladder to the tiny bridge, he bowed gravely: 'Welcome aboard, ma'am—and if you would care to take the wheel—'

'Thank you, my Captain,' she whispered and rested her head against his shoulder, this man who was to be her husband, her lover and her whole world.

Above their heads, the winter sky turned incandescent under myriad stars, a blessing upon these two who must soon put out to sea. With the strength and power of their love, the faith and hope that united them, they could sail fearlessly into whatever the future held. Over the wheel, their lips met.

For ever—and ever.

Till all the seas run dry.

The romantic gift for Christmas

First time in paperback, four superb romances by favourite authors, in an attractive special gift pack. A superb present to give. And to receive.

United Kingdom £3.80
Publication 14th October 1983

Darkness of the Heart
Charlotte Lamb

Virtuous Lady
Madeleine Ker

Lost in Summer Madness
Carole Mortimer

Man-Hater
Penny Jordan

ook for this gift pack where you buy Mills & Boon romances

Mills & Boon.
The rose of romance.